No human involved

No
Human
Involved

BARBARA SERANELLA

St. Martin's Press
New York

A THOMAS DUNNE BOOK.
An imprint of St. Martin's Press.

NO HUMAN INVOLVED. Copyright © 1997 by Barbara Seranella. All
rights reserved. Printed in the United States of America. No part of
this book may be used or reproduced in any manner whatsoever
without written permission except in the case of brief quotations
embodied in critical articles or reviews. For information, address St.
Martin's Press, 175 Fifth Avenue, New York, N.Y. 10010.

Design by Ellen R. Sasahara

Library of Congress Cataloging-in-Publication Data

Seranella, Barbara.
    No human involved / Barbara Seranella.—1st ed.
        p.   cm.
    "A Thomas Dunne Book."
    ISBN 0-312-15614-6
    I. Title
PS3569.E66N6   1997
813'.54—dc21   97-6265
                                                  CIP

First edition: August 1997

10 9 8 7 6 5 4 3 2 1

ACKNOWLEDGMENTS

I would like to thank the following persons who helped in the creation of this novel:

Ex-homicide detective Mike Walker, who shared many stories with me and a few pictures. Los Angeles Sheriff's Department Homicide Detectives Gil Carrillo and Frank Gonzales, and Senior Criminalist Elizabeth Devine who invited me into their world and took the time to show me around. My thanks also to Sheriff's Officer Mando Guzman who let me ride with him for a day in the front seat; the Palm Leaf Corporation and all the boys/men who love trains; and the fighters and trainers at Westminister Gym.

The writing of this book would not have been possible without the excellent, gentle guidance of Susan Segal, my writing mentor; my agent, Sheree Bykofsky; and my editor, Ruth Cavin.

Last, but not least, I want to thank my husband, Ron, whose loving support gave me the biggest gift a writer can hope for: *Time*. I had the motive but he supplied the opportunity.

No human involved

I

———

Buy you a drink?"

Munch turned to size up the man who spoke to her. His sad, baggy eyes were set in a basset hound face. A five o'clock shadow rolled in and out of the loose folds of skin on his cheeks and chins. Deep lines creased his forehead. She squinted a little to bring him into focus, then looked at her glass. There was only ice left.

What the hell. She shrugged an indifferent acceptance.

"Jack Daniel's, black label." She always said, "black label" when she ordered. She didn't know what it meant or if it was any better that any other colored label, but she liked the way it sounded.

The man pulled a worn leather wallet out of his back pocket. He extracted a twenty and put it on the bar. He held up two fingers to Benny, the bartender, and the money was swept away.

"What's your name?" the sad-eyed man asked.

She glanced at the fancy bottles stacked against the mirror behind the bar. "Sherry," she told him. "How's that? And we'll call you John."

"Sounds fair enough."

His skin was sallow, even in the dark and forgiving rouged light that reflected off the bottles of liquor. She thought he looked tired, beaten down. The calculation that followed was automatic.

Taking into account his age, his clothes, and the bulge in his wallet, she knew he'd probably go thirty—enough for a spoon, a six-pack, and a bag of Fritos. Not that she was interested. That part of her life was over. She was getting a fresh start, beginning today. He smiled at her. Maybe even an extra twenty, she amended, making her mouth curve upward, if he were stupid enough to leave his pants in the room when he went to the bathroom. The man collected his change, and while his attention was diverted, she took a second long look. At least he wasn't old. She hated it when they were old. It took them forever.

The negotiations would begin after the second drink, each of them speaking in carefully coached phrases.

She had once been busted for telling a middle-aged man in a Chrysler that she had a place. That was all that she'd said. "I got a place." It was right after he had asked her if she was looking for a date.

"Everybody's got a place, don't they?" she had protested as the vice cop slid the handcuffs on. They hadn't even discussed a price or service to be performed.

The cop had just shaken his head. "Save it for the judge," he said.

Supposedly if you asked them if they were a cop, they had to tell you, or they couldn't not tell you—something about entrapment. She'd never put much stock in that theory; it was probably just some hooker myth. Not a hard-and-fast rule like "Always get the money first."

"I'll buy the next round," she said. One drink and some of these guys think they own you.

He blinked slowly and his mouth dropped open. It reminded her of one of those lizards they show close up on *National Geographic* specials—lashless lids closing over dry eyeballs. It pleased her that she had surprised him.

"Whatever you say, Sherry."

Maybe he thought that she'd get so drunk, she'd do him for free. That wasn't going to happen, not today. Just one more for

2

the road and she was out of there. She'd already gone ten hours with no dope, eight of which were on purpose. It wasn't much, but it was a start, and certainly longer than she'd ever gone when she had a choice.

Benny set down two fresh cocktail napkins. She smiled when she recognized the red-white-and-blue coasters. He had bought them last year to celebrate the Bicentennial. In his patriotic zeal, he had purchased an entire gross. Cases of them were still stacked to the ceiling in the storeroom. Someone had suggested that he stock the bathrooms with them. He was a vet, he said, and he didn't think that would be right. But Lincoln's birthday? The irony wasn't lost on her. The Venture Inn catered to a color-conscious crowd. You wouldn't think Abraham Lincoln would rank as one of their heroes.

"Honoring dead Presidents, are we?" she asked him.

"Always, doll," Benny said as he slammed down their drinks. She picked up her glass before the liquor had a chance to settle.

The life had been fun once, when she was young and fresh. Sex had never been sacred, just an easy means to an easy end. "Just let them catch you," she was advised early on, "that's all a woman has to do, and the money flows in." It flowed out just as easily, going to buy the only thing that ever made her feel loved. The dope had been her salvation. She loved everything about smack. Her daily ritual began with the biting sulfur of the matches when she cooked the heroin, followed by the brown earth smell of it boiling. Those distinctive aromas heightened the pleasure, filled her with an aching anticipation. Occasionally, she used with some dope fiends who threw up at that juncture, leaving the rest of the process to her able hands. Every step so critical: dropping the little wad of cotton into the steaming brew, being careful not to splash; placing the point of the needle in the center of the makeshift filter, making sure that the opening of the point was facedown before she drew the dope up. She had once seen some old prison movie on TV. In the execution scene at the end, they showed how the bag of cyanide dropped into a vat of liquid; then

3

the gas had filled the chamber. It made her squirm, watching that.

She massaged an abscess on her forearm and winced at the tenderness of the damaged flesh. She didn't need to look at the knot beneath her fingertips to know that the abscess was red and angry; she could feel the heat of the infection through the fabric of her blouse. The abscess was her own fault, a result of shooting barbituates when she was already too loaded to see straight, much less do a proper job of giving herself a fix. Stupid, she thought, stupid and a waste. Her whole life was a waste. It was time for a change. She'd go to the country and dry out, start over.

Her arms resembled battlefields where bloody wars had been lost. Now, it was like striking oil when she found a vein, the process becoming more and more difficult. She never minded the sting of the needle; in fact, she welcomed it. Like the scorch of straight whiskey when it hit the back of her throat, she saw it as a sort of payment in advance for the pleasure to come. A quick jab to puncture a rolling vein on the top of her wrist and then victory. The rush of relief as the thick red blood spurted back into the syringe to mix with the dope, turning it all a muddy color. Then squeeze the plunger slowly, sending the precious elixir through her bloodstream. Eyes closed, she pictured the dope's path, flowing through every vein, artery, and capillary till it reached her scalp, the tips of her toes, and that dark screaming place in her gut that needed to be quieted.

"Been here long?" the sad-eyed man asked.

His voice cut into her thoughts, startled her. She'd forgotten he was there with his tired face and too many questions.

"Too long." She shook her head, angry at the way her thoughts had turned. Less than one full day clean and she was already mooning over it like some jilted lover. She knew from previous experience what to expect. The first three days would be the worst. Her bones would ache and the cravings would consume her, canceling out every other thought. She'd gone through it all before. Periodically, she would taper off. Unchecked addiction gets expensive, the habit snowballs, growing steadily, till it might cost

4

as much as seventy dollars a day just to get even, never mind high. But those times, she hadn't quit so completely, only cut down, supplementing the smaller amounts of heroin with pills and booze till her tolerance decreased. This time would be different.

The funny thing about dope was that she hadn't thought the high was anything special at first. Kind of a dreamy, sleepy numbness. It hadn't really gotten good till she was strung out. The monster was a sneaky bastard.

She scratched at the scabs on her forearms. Soon she'd be able to wear short sleeves again. She wouldn't have to cover the tattoos of needle marks running from wrist to armpit. She might even buy some new clothes, something that fit. The pants from the Salvation Army donation box were three sizes too big. She didn't spend money on anything but dope unless she absolutely had to.

She was ready to admit it: The life wasn't fun anymore. Like everything and everyone else, it had turned on her. They didn't stop for her anymore on Venice Boulevard, not even on Main Street. The men cruised past slowly in their Cadillacs and Continentals; even the Mexicans in the pickup trucks passed her by. They avoided her bold stares in search of fresher game. The dope had stopped working, too. It wasn't that the drugs were too weak or that she had been burned. All the physical signs were still there. Her eyes would take on an eerie dull shine, like a pair of those Duncan yo-yos that glowed in the dark—a flag to the narcs who circled the neighborhood. Her nose still itched and her pupils still pinned, shrinking to tiny dots. But it seemed that no matter how much dope she did, the old magic was gone. The antsy unnamed need, the hole in her gut, remained.

She turned to the man sitting next to her and said fiercely, "I'm putting down." She didn't expect him to understand. If he knew her, he wouldn't believe her. No one ever believed a hype could be anything but a hype. Fuck 'em.

"Cheers." She finished her drink and banged the bar top with an open palm. "Two more, Benny." When she saw the bartenders hesitation, she added, "For the road."

She knew Benny kept close track of his patrons' limits. He ran a tight operation, avoiding trouble when he could. He never let the jukebox play a maudlin love song near closing time; it put people in a fighting mood. When a biker got rowdy, Benny was right there. He'd clamp a warning hand on the guy's shoulder and grin him out of it. Behind that grin was a sawed-off baseball bat. Benny stayed friendly as long as he could.

"You never want to insult a drunk in front of his friends," Benny told her once. "It makes them do stupid things. Things that can get your scalp laid open."

He preferred to keep the mood upbeat. He was Irish when he wanted to be and now sang in a gravelly brogue as he poured two more whiskeys. "For the road, little darlin'."

She reached in the pocket of her baggy corduroy coat and pulled out a wad of bills. Finding a ten among the fives and ones, she paid for the drinks.

"Straight up, Benny."

Benny threw the ice he had already filled her glass with behind his back like spilled salt.

"Free ice for everybody," he yelled. The bikers playing pool swore at him affectionately. Benny laughed and sprayed seltzer in the air over his head. He shook his long beard and shaggy head of curls as the mist fell into them. He looked like one of those characters in a Disney movie—the goofy professor who accidentally crosses himself with a dog. Benny was a standard poodle in a black motorcycle jacket.

She pulled a Lucky Strike from the other pocket of her coat. Benny leaned toward her with his lighter. John beat him to it.

She grabbed his hand to steady the match.

"Thanks."

He shook the match out and let it drop to the floor. It sputtered amid the beer and sawdust.

"I just came in to square up my account. I'm getting out of here," she said, almost to herself.

"Why?" the man at her elbow asked.

She studied him for a while before answering, choosing her words. "I don't want to be dead anymore." She pointed to their reflections in the mirror behind the bar. "Look at us. Do you see any sign of life?" Rubbing a finger across the black circles under her eyes, she said, "I look like a zombie." She leaned toward him as if to share a confidence, "Dope is poison."

He didn't seem surprised; maybe he didn't get it.

"I shouldn't be telling you this." She downed the bourbon in one wincing gulp and dropped her voice to a whisper. "I'm a junkie." Raising her glass in a toast, she corrected herself. "Was," she said. Empty glass still raised, she tried to get Benny's attention, but his back was turned to her.

"What happened?" the man asked quietly, swinging her attention back to his direction.

"What happened?" Her face twisted in on itself as she struggled to find the words to explain. She let the pain show through her eyes, letting her guard down for a stranger she'd never see again. "I'll tell you what happened. I didn't notice till this morning. I was in a bathroom." She spent a lot of time in bathrooms, usually with the door locked, crouched on the floor, with a tie on her arm. She didn't tell him that part. "Bright lights and a big mirror over the sink. I looked at myself, really looked, and it was like a veil lifted for a second. I'm dying here." She confronted her newfound confidant in the mirror.

"Look at you. You got it, too. Look at your face. You're all wrinkled and sad. Are you happy? Is it worth it, what you do?"

"Sometimes, not always." He went back to his drink, but she saw he still watched her. A steady, dead eye locked on her over the rim of his bucket glass. Maybe there was hope for him, too.

She grabbed his arm. "Let's get out of here."

"Where would we go?"

"To the country. I'm sick of the city. The city's poison, too."

"You'll need money."

"I've got enough for what I need to do." She slapped the bar again. "Benny, my man, another one. Then I gotta go."

7

The bartender walked over to where she sat. He planted his hands firmly on the bar, palms down, and waited till she had to look at him.

She sucked it in and put on a show of sobriety. "Last one, I promise."

Benny considered, then relented with a hoarse Wolfman Jack laugh. "The road is calling," he sang out.

John put a hand over his glass and shook his head. Benny turned to other customers.

A thin youth snuck into the bar, casting furtive glances toward the bartender's direction, and sidled up to her. The boy's wary eyes darted to the bikers playing pool and then back to her. Oily blond hair fell to his collar. The stingy growth of a first mustache glistened with beads of sweat on his upper lip. "Where's Flower George?" he asked her, drawing the sleeve of his T-shirt across his mouth.

"I don't know." She pushed the boy away. "Why d'ya ask me? Screw him."

"I'm out of flowers. He promised me." The boy wiped his palms on his jeans. "I haven't had any *flowers* all day." His voice took on an extra note of urgency when he said the word *flowers*.

"Time to get out of the *flower* business, kid." She turned her back on the boy.

"Who's this George? Your boyfriend?" her drinking companion asked. "I'm not going to have some jealous biker sticking a gun in my face, am I?"

"Flower George is an old man. You don't have to worry about him."

"How old are *you*, Sherry?"

"Twenty-one." She raised her glass to Benny. "Or I wouldn't be here, right?"

"That's right, sugar." Benny's liquor license was on probation for serving underaged girls. He had to be careful whom he let in, even though it broke his black Irish heart to turn away the succulent young things who came to the Venture Inn in search of thrills.

"Tell me about George."

She swirled her keys in the dimes of water standing on the thick lacquer of the bar top. Drawing the water into lines, she watched as the tiny rivulets returned to the mother puddle. Eventually, she broke off a drop of water that quivered alone. "Hotel California" played on the jukebox.

"What's to tell? He sells flowers. I don't know where he gets them—probably picks them in the country somewhere." She looked down as she spoke and let her lips go slack. "He drives this big white van full of flowers. He gives them to the kids to sell. You know, the kids who stand on the corners with those five-gallon plastic buckets. You gotta keep the flowers in water. They still don't last. The city murders them."

"What was that you said?" He leaned closer. She could see the red veins in his sad, tired eyes. "I didn't hear the last part."

"It's a good business." She sat upright and patted the wad in her pocket. "All cash."

"Is he mean to the kids? Did he beat you?"

"He's old—did I tell you that? Old men are a pain in the ass. You know what I mean? He's always asking me, 'Is it hard yet?' " She mimicked, making a face with downturned mouth and peering eyes. " 'Am I in?' "

The man pulled away from her, blinking faster. She knew she had shocked him, and that realization spurred her on.

"He didn't even know when he was hard. I mean, why bother? Right? How do you know when it's over?" At some point, it should be over. She noticed the glass in her hand. How had it emptied so quickly? She had meant to stop there only for a moment. She had planned to pay Benny what she owed him, square her debt, and then hit the road. Then he had bought her a drink to say thank you; she had bought another to say you're welcome. She turned to her companion, "Hey, it sure has gotten drunk out."

A flash of blue intersected the red lights reflected in the mirror over the bar. Sirens whined on their way to the Oakwood Projects, "Ghost Town" to the locals. The bar door swung open and a shaft of light made it to the back wall before being extinguished. Motes of dust swirled in the rays of the setting sun. Soon the light would be gone, marking the midway point of another lost weekend in Venice.

She caught a glimpse of the activity on the street in the mirror and realized that she had stayed way too long. "I gotta use the head. Save my place."

After she got up, Benny emptied the ashtray she had used and spoke to her companion from the side of his mouth. "Stay away from her, man," Benny growled in his borderline laryngitis. "She's hot."

"Hot?"

"She's got the clap. She won't do nothing about it."

The hound-faced man waited a few minutes, alternately watching the doors and the entrance to the bathrooms. His shoulders hunched forward in an attitude of indifference to his surroundings, but his eyes took in everything around him: Thickly tattooed bikers played pool and postured for one another; leather-clad women hung on their men's arms, glaring at one another under heavily made-up lids. There was a Confederate flag tacked to the far wall. By the door, a sign that read NO NIGGERS hung next to a dartboard full of bullet holes.

He nodded to a man in a blue knit stocking cap and a three-day growth of beard who was leaning against the wall. The man stood up and ambled toward the bathrooms.

"Shit," Detective Mace St. John swore when he glanced down at the bar top and noticed that her keys were gone.

MUNCH emptied the pockets of the big coat, taking only what she absolutely needed, and left the bulky jacket on the floor of the bathroom. The coat was too cumbersome and she needed to move fast. She crawled out the tiny window and dropped behind the Dumpster in the parking lot. A bolt of fiery agony shot up her shin when she hit the ground. Her mouth went dry as a surge of adrenaline dried up the pain.

She had to think. Damn it. She needed a clear head.

Deafening noise filled the alley that ran behind the bar. Into the back parking lot, twelve members of the Satan's Pride Motorcycle Club arrived en masse. Their colors were vivid patches of red and black sewn on cutoff Levi vests. *Satan's Pride MC* on the top banner and *Venice, California* down below. The center logo was a biker astride a '58 panhead, a woman's head in his hand. He was holding the head by its hair and the woman was screaming. In the background were flames.

The Harleys roared a thundering finale. The bikers gunned their engines till flames shot out the back of their illegal straight pipes; somewhere, a car alarm went off. Unsmiling, they shut off their choppers. The ole ladies untied their hair and waited while their men chained their bikes together.

Munch crawled till she reached the corner of the brick wall. Carefully, she poked her head around and stole a look at the front entrance. Three men shone long black flashlights through the windows of the van. Cops. She'd been stupid to drive the van there.

She crawled to the other end of the parking lot and took off down the alley.

DETECTIVE Sgt. Mace St. John pulled a pen out of his shirt pocket. He tilted the glass that had held her drink over and, without touching the surface, dropped it into a plain brown paper bag that he extracted from his pocket. Then he dated and initialed the front of the bag and wrote a short description of the contents.

Benny watched wordlessly, rubbing down the bar top and drying glasses with the same terry-cloth rag he used for everything.

St. John threw a five on the bar to cover the cost of the glass and asked for a receipt.

The detective gave a slow, disgusted blink and shook his head. He'd misjudged her. He was slipping. He waited for the undercover officer in the blue knit cap to come back inside.

The man hung back till Mace gestured for him to join him.

"We lost her."

"I figured. Little rug rat like that probably knows these alleys inside and out. Let's get out of here."

They walked out front. A tow truck driver was waiting for the fingerprint man to finish dusting the driver's door handle of a white van.

"Open it," the detective instructed. The tow truck driver coaxed the driver's side door lock up with a slim-jim. "Just the steering wheel, and then get it out of here." He turned to a second cop. "Does the ME have anything for us?"

"Nothing more than the obvious. Cause of death: murder by gunshot wounds to the head. He sent the bullets to Ballistics."

"No rush." Mace held up the evidence bag. "Let's get a make on these prints so we can match them to the ones in the vehicle and the house." He looked down the alley. "The girl's a hype. She won't go far."

"What do you want to do now, Sarge?"

"Let's go back to the house for a final look." Mace checked his watch. It was almost six o'clock.

The call had come in at noon. A black-and-white responded to the hysterical call that there had been a shooting on Brooks. Uniformed officers investigated and called in a code 187, murder to find. An easy determination. No suicide ever managed to place six rounds in his own face. St. John was on call that weekend and scheduled to receive whatever murder case came along. He hadn't made any other plans; chances had been high he'd catch a case. Tensions between the all-black Shoreline Crips and Chicano V-13 gangs had been building. With Valentine's Day right around the corner, they could expect a jump in domestics, as well. He knew that sometimes the murder stats jump for no apparent reason. Different guys had their theories. Some blamed the full moon, a sudden heat wave, whatever. You get a week where the city just erupts. Who can say for sure what brings it on? This week was starting off badly and the weather was still cool.

By 1:30, he was at the death scene, wearing an old pair of slacks and a sweat-stained T-shirt. The dispatcher reached him at the gym, where he'd spent the morning sparring and preparing his protégé, a bantamweight seventeen-year-old fresh off the street, for an upcoming bout. The good fighters never come from between clean sheets; Digger had taught him that.

St. John's shield hung on a thin chain around his neck; his service revolver was concealed under his windbreaker. He arrived at the house in an unmarked Chevrolet. A group of teenagers huddled across the street, mostly white kids. When the detective approached them, they scattered like cockroaches.

Flower George's house was on the fringe of Ghost Town. It was a low stucco building that squatted ungracefully next to abandoned Pacific Electric tracks. Graffiti blackened the walls and the sheets of plywood that were nailed over the window frames. The house was surrounded by a chain-link fence with a foot of indestructible fast-food wrappers woven into the bottom of it. An assortment of bald tires and beer bottles littered the front yard. Mace ordered the yellow tape to be strung. He climbed the stairs of the front porch, past the dying, anemic clumps of dandelions and foxtails that had surrendered to the city soot, and went inside.

He stepped over the two-by-four nailed to the hardwood floor in the entry hall, part of a homegrown barricade system. The board was approximately the same width as the plank of wood leaning against the doorjamb. Once the door was shut and the board in place, this would be a very difficult house to enter. It hadn't made it any safer for the body lying inside.

Inside job, he thought.

He walked down the dark hallway. His flashlight revealed a

mattress on the floor of every dirty room. The body was in the third room he entered. A uniformed cop stood at the doorway. St. John nodded to the officer and went inside. The corpse was naked and turning light yellow as the blood drained to the lowest point in the body. It smelled of vomit and excrement, not all of it fresh. The detective pulled a jar of Vicks mentholated jelly out of his pocket and generously swathed each nostril. He offered some to the cop in the doorway and the man accepted it gratefully.

Mace studied the face, what was left of it. The right socket was empty. The detective's flashlight found a glass eye in the corner of the room. The startled eyeball stared back at him from a nest of spiderwebs and burned matches. He counted the entry wounds. They were made by a small-caliber bullet and were grouped close together. Probably a .22, fired at close range. Small coronas of powder burns tattooed the jaundiced skin.

Mace's new partner, Detective Patrolman Tony Cassiletti, joined him. Together, they stood over the body; an expression of revulsion twisted the younger man's face.

"Welcome to the glamour of Homicide," St. John said, and handed Cassiletti the blue jar of balm.

Cassiletti asked, "What do you make of it?"

"I'd say the perp was very pissed off." The rookie nodded thoughtfully, as if his superior had just provided him with some deep insight.

"Look at this." Cassiletti lifted the sheet draped over the victim's foot. There was a tattoo on the sole of the left foot. It read: *Hang it here, motherfucker.* An arrow pointed to a dotted line in blue around the big toe. "Here's one for your collection, Sarge."

Mace took a picture of the tattoo. "Another fine upstanding citizen." He straightened and arched his back. Planting a palm at the base of his spine, he stifled a yawn with the back of his other hand. "We got a name yet?"

Cassiletti consulted his notepad. His hands shook. Mace noted the high color in his cheeks. Cassiletti was new to the detail, a recent transfer from City Hall security, serving the mayor at campaign dinners. The most action he had probably seen was the subduing of a drunk at a United Way fund-raiser. "Full name: George Mancini, aka 'Flower George.' He had a record: pandering, contributing, small-time dealer. Looks like whoever croaked him did the world a favor."

Mace smiled at the younger man. Sounded like Cassiletti had been watching too many movies.

The background check revealed a Ford Econoline van registered to the deceased. The van was also missing. "Put out an APB on the van. Call me if it shows up." Mace made a note of the plate number. "Any witnesses?" he asked the cop in the doorway.

The man laughed. "Yeah, as soon as we come up with the perp, we'll have twenty slimebags ready to do their civic duty and say they saw him twenty miles away all morning."

"Her," Mace said, looking at the cluster of bullet holes. "The shooter will be a her. A guy would fire two rounds, three tops, even in a rage. We're looking for a very angry lady."

The van was spotted four hours later at the Venture Inn, a biker dive at the end of Venice Boulevard. It had been almost too easy, until the girl eluded them.

Mace watched the van lumber off on the hook of the tow truck. He sighed. The lieutenant wasn't going to be happy. St. John consoled himself with the thought that in a day, it would be forgotten. When the girl's identity was confirmed, he'd issue a warrant for her arrest. Within the month, they'd probably pick her up on something else. If they were lucky, her prints would catch up with her while she was still in custody. There was always a chance she'd make it out on her own recognizance, but they'd bust her again. She wasn't going far; that type never did. He made a note to himself to post her picture in the squad room and give a copy to Vice, too. This one was going down.

"I think what we got here is a clear case of AVA, NHI," St. John said.

Cassiletti looked confused.

"Asshole versus asshole," Mace translated, "no human involved." He grinned at the rookie detective. "What say we call it a day?"

The other cop nodded and looked relieved. Mace guessed that he probably had someone waiting for him at home, worrying about him. It was easier to have no one. He'd figure that out for himself.

2

Munch stayed off the surface streets. When she was almost to the end of the alley, she started cutting through backyards. She vaulted over and under fences before the pit bulls and Dobermans had a chance to come fully to their feet. Along the way, she pulled clothes off of lines and clutched them to her chest.

She ran till her legs turned to rubber and she couldn't grab enough breath to fill her aching lungs. When she spotted a two-foot opening under the wooden stairs of a back porch, she dived inside. As the panic subsided, she felt pain: a prickly burning in her ankle, sharp stabs in her thighs and sides. She was out of adrenaline.

The house where she sought refuge was a typical Venice bungalow gone to seed: wood-shingled and at one time painted white. Empty window boxes now hung lopsided and forgotten beneath windows with burglar bars. The white paint was peeling in long blistered strips and the wood had been chewed into curling tunnels by industrious termites. Lying in the fine gray dust under the back porch, she imagined herself invisible.

In the kitchen above her, chairs scraped across the floor. Forks clattered on stoneware plates. A refrigerator door opened and closed. The people in the house were talking, but she couldn't make out individual words. She willed herself to take only shallow, quiet breaths.

She waited till they finished eating and then another half an hour of silence before daring to stir. Her clothes were damp with sweat and resisted her efforts to shed them. The dirt under the house clung to her, as well. Slowly, she pulled on the pants she had stolen. They fit better than the pair she would leave behind. She tied a red bandanna around her head. It seemed to take forever for night to come and the whiskey haze to lift.

The battle with the monster had begun. Getting loaded would only make things worse. She counted all the reasons she shouldn't use, starting with the obvious danger of clouding her mind when she needed every faculty clear and operating at maximum. No sooner did she get that settled, decide her course, than that little message would return: A taste would help. Just a little taste to take the edge off. God, she thought, no wonder when people off themselves, they shoot their heads.

It took another twenty minutes of slinking through alleys to reach the cab depot on Electric Avenue. She found Wizard working on the brakes of an old two-toned Checker. Wizard lived his entire life, as had she, within the borders of Venice. He'd always managed to stay uninvolved with gang rivalries. None of his neighbors ever gave him grief. Only the nappy head of white hair and the deep crease above the bridge of his nose betrayed his years. The muscles under his raisin black skin were as hard as onyx. She had once seen him park a Volkswagon by picking up the rear end by its bumper and setting it next to the curb. His real name was Orson Ozwald. In a world where few people ever went by their given name, Ozwald became Oz. His expertise with a cutting torch had earned him the respected title of "the Wizard." She was his apprentice. The crowd she ran with called her whatever they wanted to, "Little Bit," mostly. Since she'd worked with Oz, her childhood nickname was revived. Now they called her Munch, short for munchkin.

"Wizard," she hissed to him from the shadows.

His hand was halfway to his buck knife before he recognized her.

"What's up, girl?" He took in the brightness of her eyes. "You're not here to work, are you?"

"I want to buy that GTO."

"You got cash?"

She pulled the wad from her pocket and counted three hundred dollars into his palm.

He shook his head and clucked his tongue. "What you done now, girl?" Before she could answer, he held up his palm, a startling white flag of calloused skin. "I don't want to know. I'll get the keys."

She clung to the shadows while he went to his Peg-Board. "Uh, Wizard . . ."

"Don't worry, I haven't seen you." He threw her the keys and went back to his brake job. "The pink slip is under the seat."

"I know."

"Git outta here." She nodded and slipped out the side gate.

The Pontiac had a quarter of a tank of gas. She counted what was left of her funds: fourteen dollars. Enough for a dime bag and a couple of packs of smokes. No, she was putting down. No dope, no alcohol for a while, either. She'd been stupid to get drunk.

Her bones were starting to ache; she could feel it even through the booze. That's why they called it "the monster." It's ugly when it turns on you. Your nose starts to run when the first tide of withdrawal sweeps over you. There's a perverted pride that goes along with the amount you suffer. Like you must be some kind of good to have it together enough to have a really big habit going. When she'd been in jail, some black girl with a blond wig had strutted back and forth in the misdemeanor tank, bragging that she was a good whore. Munch had lain on her cot, covered with a thin wool blanket, teeth chattering, but not from the air conditioning, and decided that she must be an excellent dope fiend.

She rubbed her brow, wishing she could shut her eyes against the bright lights of the oncoming traffic. It would be so easy, she thought, to give the wheel a sudden turn into the other lane. No, she told herself, then *he* would win.

Her muscles ached and her skin felt raw. She tried to pretend she had the flu. She was sick now, she told herself, but the feeling would pass. Her hair hurt. She checked the rearview mirror and avoided looking into her own eyes.

Give it up, a little voice said. You know you're going to give in eventually. Why wait?

An insidious debate began. The longer she waited, the worse it would get, the voice promised her. All her actions were predicated on the fragile belief that she stood a chance. Her resolve must not flicker or she would be lost.

"I'm sick," she said out loud.

You've always given in in the past, the voice responded.

A flu with dialogue, she amended. A treacherous, will-corroding kind of flu she'd always done anything, said anything, sold anything to cure. Until now. Especially now, when she knew exactly what it would take to cure her, to get her even again. The second wave would be much worse, adding debilitation to the craving. She'd given in at that stage before, sweating and sniffling, unable to sleep. Turning a trick is agony, especially if the guy expects you to act friendly. The car beside her honked as she realized that she had strayed into the other lane.

Focus, she told herself. You're not beat yet.

She wiped her nose with her sleeve and headed for Sepulveda Boulevard. She wasn't in jail now, and if she hoped to stay that way, she'd better move. Sybil Brand Institute for Women was an experience Munch had vowed never to repeat. Until then, cops and robbers had been a big game, one she always felt she had the edge on. The cops arrested her, she gave them a name, spent a night in jail, and then got released on her own recognizance the next morning after promising to return for court. She was so slick, until the day came when she found out that she had only been putting off the inevitable.

She knew the point system by which they determined who

qualified for OR like other kids knew their multiplication tables. If you lived at the same address for over two years, that was a couple of points. If you had a job, three more. Two points each for family in the area and if the crime was a first offense. They never checked the information she gave them, just filled out the appropriate blanks on their forms and tallied the points. She told them just enough to qualify each time and laughed all the way to the street. Usually, she'd be in the cooker within the hour.

They'd keep her this time.

She turned north, toward the Sepulveda pass. The road took her past the Veterans Administration and cemetery. She glanced at the endless rows of white tombstones, momentarily mesmerized by their shifting, neat patterns.

This would be much worse than the November eleventh bust, which was her fifth "first offense." The possession charge had been bogus. All she'd had were fresh needle marks, but they called it "internal possession of a controlled substance," which made the marks a felony and meant an automatic seventy-two-hour hold. Long enough for all the other charges to catch up with her and all the other aliases she had ever used to be tied together with her fingerprints. That time, there had been no release on her own recognizance.

The San Diego freeway raged beside her. The traffic sounds poured in her open window. She heard sirens from behind her and looked for the source of those wails in her rearview mirror. They were getting closer, yelping and honking. Two Highway Patrol cars screamed past her on the freeway to her left. She remembered the expired tags on the Pontiac and the driver's license in her pocket that she dared not use. Surely, they had her name by now.

She turned her attention back to the road in front of her.

Sepulveda wound under the freeway and through the mountains, mountains that had been carved out and filled in. They were building a golf course there someday on top of the dump. She'd seen golf courses on TV before. They had trees and lakes and everybody talked in low, soothing voices. She'd like to see one, to lie under a blue sky on the sweet-smelling grass and watch the clouds blow over her. Just once before—no, she wasn't going to die yet. Fuck 'em all. George used to say, "Fuck 'em all but seven. Six pallbearers and a motorcycle cop." Thinking about George gave her a second wind. A hot rush of hate filled her. The son of a bitch had made her a murderer.

Fuck 'em twice, she thought. I don't care. She wished she could she could just turn it all off. Just a taste, the message echoed. Her hands tightened on the steering wheel. No, not now. Did that mean later? She forced herself to stay within the speed limit.

She knew about the landfill because she'd been there with Wizard to dump scrap. They had gone at night. She had asked him what was on the other side of the mountain.

"The San Fernando Valley," he had told her. It sounded romantic.

"Is the country that way?"

"The country's farther out, Little Bit."

He had laughed at her. Maybe he thought she'd never get to the country, but she would. She'd have a horse, and some chickens even. She crested the hill and came to a light where the Mulholland overpass spanned the freeway. Eight lanes of citizens flowed both ways. Crazy Mike, the president of the Satan's Pride, had also taken her here. He had spat on the shiny cars driving home, driving to work. They were fools, he said. Following all their citizens rules, allowing themselves to be herded through life. They didn't know how to live like scooter trash did. Of course, he was talking about the brothers, not the women. Ninety-nine percent of the population were citizens, Crazy Mike said, only 1 percent were outlaws—the lucky 1 percent who lived by no rules. His words had been a lie. There were many laws in the world of bikers, the breaking of which was sometimes punishable by death. Crazy Mike had bragged wildly that night about the glory of the club. Then they had crossed the overpass and returned to Venice, where he had raped her before he gave his brothers their turns.

She shoved aside the memory. There was nothing she could do about that now.

The light changed and she pushed on. Sepulveda went under a tunnel, dark and cool. A car heading south honked its horn. She blotted at the sweat on her forehead. "All right, all right," she chanted, "so far, so good." She took her foot off the gas pedal and coasted down the grade to conserve fuel.

On her right, she watched the valley prepare for night. Lights blinked on in the homes and businesses. The magnitude of the city below awed her—a rainbow of colors, like Christmas lights, that went on for miles. It looked like a place that a person could get lost in.

She felt the shift in the tempo of the motor before the idiot lights lit up the dash. First the red light that read OIL flashed on and then the one that read GEN. The steering got stiff and she didn't have to try the brakes to know that the power assist would be gone. The engine had stalled, and it shouldn't have. The hum from the motor had been consistent the entire drive up the grade. The drone of it had harmonized through her brain, directly through her clenched teeth, all the way to her skull. If it had missed a beat, she would have known it, been forewarned. Now it had died suddenly and completely. The silence was horrifying, especially now, running for her life for the first time she had ever allowed herself to care enough to try. George would have said that only fools care.

She let the car coast while it still had the downhill momentum and forced herself to coldly consider her options. The gas gauge still registered an eighth of a tank. She turned off the key but left the headlights on, then looked for a place to go to ground as the big car plummeted down Sepulveda.

The canyon road twisted in ways she was helpless to anticipate. The city lights mocked her now on the right beyond sheer cliffs. She was going too fast to take the turns and stay in her lane. The tires screamed as she corrected and fought the stiff steering to stay on the paved surface. She didn't want to draw unneces-

23

sary attention to herself, so she risked a tap on the brake pedal. It was stiff and unyielding. She put both feet on the brake and leaned into the seat. The wheel twisted in her hands and for twenty yards, two wheels rode in the dirt shoulder. Finally, she started to slow, sacrificing precious momentum for safety. There was still no shelter in sight, just chain-linked fences that came all the way out to the road. A sharp curve loomed ahead.

"Help me," she demanded, to whom she didn't know.

The Pontiac rounded the curve. A dirt turnout sheltered by a hedge of overgrown oleanders and bottlebrushes appeared on the right. She rolled beneath the shaggy branches. She kept going till the car was swallowed by the foliage; then she put both feet on the brake and pushed with all the thrust her hundred pounds could deliver. The car finally stopped at the base of a brick retaining wall. The five-mile-per-hour impact was enough to shatter a headlight and flatten the grille. Somewhere a dog barked, but no lights came on in the big houses around her. She put the car in park and cranked the motor. It turned over too fast, as if the compression was low. Shit, she thought, the timing gear must have stripped.

There was nothing left to do. She curled into a ball and waited for morning. She slept once, briefly, and dreamed she was shooting dope and Flower George was laughing at her.

3

That night, a weary Mace St. John climbed aboard the platform of the Bella Donna and locked the wrought-iron gate after him. He rummaged around in his refrigerator. On the bottom shelf, he found eggs and mayonnaise, but he soon discovered that he was out of bread. He grabbed a bottle of olives and the plastic bag behind them. Opening the overhead cabinet, he selected a box of Ritz crackers and decided they would suffice. He should have gotten something to eat while he was out; it was too much hassle to cook for just himself.

With his free hand, he filled a highball glass with ice and returned to the lounge section that served as his den/living room/office. He'd faithfully restored the Santa Fe–designed, Pullman-built officer's coach till she was as close to her original 1927 condition as he could manage, right down to the brass spittoons. He had bought the car in '72 at auction. The Bella Donna had sat for three years, gathering dust while Amtrak decided her fate. When he first saw her, she had been stripped bare of most of her original appointments and was being sold for scrap. His dad and he couldn't believe their luck. Miraculously, not one stained-glass window was broken and the original chandelier still hung in the porter's kitchen.

He folded back the bar top and fixed himself a martini. Originally, the bar had been made of walnut, no doubt polished diligently each day by white-gloved porters to a mirror finish. He hadn't been able to afford the expensive hardwood and had had to make do with Philippine mahogany, which he dressed up with gilded cherubs. He'd blown his budget on the rug in the lounge, but once he'd seen the pattern in a copy of *Architectural Digest,* he'd known he would never be satisfied with anything less. The salesman at the carpet store had had to send away to New Orleans. The design was popular there, the salesman explained, commonly used in restorations of the old southern antebellum mansions. The short-napped runner with its pink and white peonies and yellowed gardenias turned out to be worth every hassle. The rich red background proved a perfect match for the velvet flocked wallpaper of the dining section. He loved the shades of green in the leaves of the flowers, a subtle range of hues from aquamarine, jade, and cucumber to good old olive drab. Every color contrasted nicely with the soothing peach of the walls.

While he fixed his drink, the plastic bag that he had retrieved from his refrigerator perspired on the bar top. He shook off the moisture and studied the bag's contents. The bag held a clump of tomato seeds, unexplained evidence recovered from a severed arm, and they were trying to tell him something—he could feel it. Maybe he should plant them. He laughed at himself noiselessly, smiling and shaking his head. Did he think they would grow like Jack's bean stalk into a vine that led him to the killer?

He busied himself with the preparation of his martini. The antique gilt-framed mirrors over the bar with the splintered silver showing through played tricks on his tired eyes. Shapes formed that made him think of the jungle. He blinked to clear the image, but all he could see was a canopy of tropical leaves blocking out the sun. So easy to lose your way in the jungle, to lose all sense of direction. He had gone days on patrol sometimes with no clear sighting of the sun, just a fade-in and fade-out of light, and tigers, fucking tigers.

He sipped his gin and thought about the girl in the bar. The hooker had been right about one thing: The city was poison. If you weren't careful, it sucked the red right out of your blood. No sense in dwelling on it; he was tied to the city as long as his dad was still around.

Digger. Shit. He better call him.

He picked up the phone and dialed the number at his dad's house, but there was no answer. Digger had probably unplugged the phone again. Mace wished he wouldn't do that. What if there were an emergency?

He listened to the dissatisfying sound of the phone ringing and thought about his dad not hearing him on the other end. In a way, he envied his dad the luxury of disconnecting. Mace always needed to be available for those 3:00 A.M. calls to crime scenes— hard on a marriage, those late-night calls.

Digger—it was just the two of them now. The old man had gotten his nickname in the army, during the "good war." Something about the speed with which he dug trenches while his brigade was stationed at Anzio, where, to hear him tell it, his unit had personally won the war. He had made war sound so romantic, like there was no greater honor than to be carried home on your shield after giving your life for your country. Pumped with patriotic dreams of glory, Mace enlisted right out of high school. Two tours in the jungle had cured him of those ideals, and when the time had come, he hadn't reenlisted.

He listened as the phone rang for the twentieth time and wondered where the years had gone. The two of them used to plan for the day when they would have the Bella Donna ready for the *big trip*. Buy a one-way ticket from Amtrak to tour the country, hitched behind a big engine, stopping where they pleased, doing all those things fathers and sons do.

Mace shook his head as if to clear it of the day's failures and life's many disappointments. He hung up the phone and sat down at the wicker table that served as his desk, dropping the bag of unexplained tomato seeds next to a manila folder. Stenciled on the folder's cover was a six-digit number; beneath the impersonal case number, he hoped sometime soon to fill in the victim's name. That might be all he could do for the dead girl; she deserved at least that much.

The press had started calling the murderer "the Ballona Creek Butcher" and had plastered the slim but sordid details of the case on the front page. The severed limb that had first been discovered by the twenty-year-old captain of the UCLA crew team had just the right measure of horror and proximity to pique the city's attention. The case quickly turned high-profile and the mayor called in downtown's major crime division, the RHD, to assist. Heading the elite unit was Mace's ex-partner, Ernie Potts. In a way, it had been like old times, the two of them together again. Ernie had an uncanny ability for sniffing out felonies. He claimed it was just a matter of getting into the criminal's head.

Mace had been the first detective to interview the crew captain. The young woman told him that she was preparing to launch her scull into Ballona Creek for morning practice when she spotted something bumping against the rocks at the base of the concrete ramp. It was the red of the nail polish that first caught her eye, she said. After she got over her initial horror, she called the police department. He remembered thinking that this was going to be a stone whodunit. He had felt a surge of excitement. This was what it was all about, a case that challenged all his ability, a guaranteed moneymaker sure to rack up lots of overtime. His second reaction—maybe it was the heart-shaped mood ring on the index finger—was resigned disgust.

After the initial brouhaha died down, the crime-scene technicians had found little else to go on and many questions remained unanswered. The file had grown no bigger since January thirty-first, and fresher crimes clamored to be solved.

The Ballona Creek case haunted Mace. Visions of that lonely arm bobbing in the water filled his thoughts in unguarded idle moments. Maybe the deceased had a family somewhere, looking for her. Then again, maybe he was a fool, spinning his wheels on a hopeless homicide. The smart thing to do would be just to let it go; he had enough cases already. But he never let go—hadn't that been one of Nan's many complaints? Mace looked out the window at the neighboring warehouses. All was quiet. The gathering darkness gentled the appearance of the surrounding lots. The cars that rotted among the weeds and broken beer bottles now appeared to be parked rather than abandoned. Even the grating he had installed over his windows to prevent the neighborhood kids from throwing rocks through the leaded glass dissolved into benign screens. The vandalism was nothing personal, he understood, just a need the kids had to mark that they had been there. Something to point to and say, "I broke that."

The track that the Bella Donna stood on was at the end of the old Southern Pacific line and ran parallel to Olympic Boulevard. The owners of the property had erected a large warehouse that they divided into cubicles and leased for self-storage. They were delighted to have a police officer guarding their investment at night and struck a deal of mutual accommodation. Mace parked his coach car free on the siding of track in their lot and they rested easier.

As Mace watched, the light on Olympic changed and two lowriders peeled off in an impromptu drag race. The cars' tires screamed as they found traction on the asphalt and the scent of burning rubber drifted over the Bella Donna and her lone occupant.

Mace turned back to the file. Officially, the case was no longer his concern. They had patted him on his head and told him to step aside and let the big boys handle this one. He was free to go back to his misdemeanor murders and drug overdoses. The mayor claimed that the purpose of RHD's intervention was to reduce the caseload of overworked divisional detectives. Mace's hand tightened on his drink as he thought of the mayor's words. One big happy family, right?

Didn't it strike any of them as odd that with all of Parker Center's resources, they still had no identity of the victim, crime

29

scene, or even cause of death? Granted, in the Butcher homicide, there wasn't much to go on. Without a complete corpse, they technically didn't even know if a homicide had been committed. They were treating this one "as if."

Mace opened the folder and quickly scanned its contents.

On the morning of January thirty-first, Mace had delivered the severed arm, wrapped in white butcher's paper, to the coroner's forensic lab. There he handed it over to Carol Zapata, who was, in his humble opinion, the best crime-scene technician available. She had injected saline into the puckered fingertips, and when they plumped back up, she took a set of prints. He'd seen her work on worse decoms, bodies buried in shallow graves, overdose victims left to rot in filthy shooting galleries and stripped of all identification. On older corpses, the skin sloughed off easily. She would cut the fingers at the second knuckle, peel off the ridged flesh, and fit the hollow fingertips of dead skin over her own surgically gloved hands. Then she would proceed as if she were printing herself. This time, that hadn't been necessary.

"You're pretty good at this," Mace had commented, always awed by her ingenuity.

"This can't have been in the water long," she had replied, smiling and blushing slightly in acknowledgment of his compliment. "Or the marine life would have nibbled the fingers to the bone." She prepared for him several petri dishes labeled with the case number. "I found sand under the nails, and vegetation. Embedded too deeply to have gotten there casually."

There had been a lot of sand in the muscle, as if it had been dredged through a dune or maybe buried and then the ground tamped down over it.

He had studied the bits of plant in the plastic container, holding them up to the fluorescent lights and asking Carol, "Any idea what this is?"

"Botany's not my thing," she had said, pausing to look directly in his eyes, inviting him to ask.

He hadn't.

The Coast Guard had done an air and sea search but had failed to recover any more pieces to the gruesome puzzle. Ballona Creek was connected by storm drains all the way to the San Gabriel Valley; point of origin would be difficult, if not impossible, to determine.

A week later, on the seventh of February, one week after the first arm had been discovered, a second arm washed up under the pier at the base of Washington Boulevard. This time, crabs had gotten to it first and gnawed away the fingertips. One thing was certain: It was a right arm, just as the first arm had been. It, too, was assigned a case number and handed over to RHD. Captain Divine told Mace in no uncertain terms that he would honor no overtime vouchers related to the Ballona case. The captain was under pressure from the city about the jump in the homicide statistics in their division. They had enough to do. "Leave it alone," he said.

Mace put his drink glass in the sink of his kitchenette, returned the bag of seeds to the refrigerator, and stumbled wearily to the front bedroom of the Bella Donna. He didn't even bother to take off his shoes. He just pulled the Murphy bed out from the wall and collapsed beneath the framed Remington prints of cowboys and Indians.

4

_____

The following morning, Mace returned to the banks of Ballona Creek. Sunday was his day off; he could spend it how he pleased. He climbed over the fence and walked the length of the waterway. When he heard a rustling in the bushes below, he realized that he wasn't alone. Twenty yards away, the top of a thick patch of bamboo parted and a woman emerged. He watched her thrash through the weeds, following a winding rivulet of two-inch-deep water that cut through the sand. She beat the bushes in front of her with a knarled walking stick, all the while mumbling to herself. An ancient Irish setter with a bandanna knotted around his throat wheezed beside her. Neither of the pair was aware of his presence.

He vaulted the chain-link fence and slid down the bank to where the woman and dog stood. As he got closer to them, he noted that the dog and the woman were well matched. The woman was older than she appeared from a distance. Her thin face was weathered and wrinkled. Mace figured that she had to be in her seventies. Worn hiking boots peeked out beneath the folds of her long gypsy skirt. On her head, she wore an ancient sunbonnet; wisps of graying red hair escaped out the sides.

"What are you looking for?" Mace asked when he was in speaking distance.

She eyed him suspiciously from beneath the brim of her hat. "You the fella the city sent?" she asked.

"I'm just taking a walk," he told her.

"Funny place just to be walking," she said. "I'm supposed to meet a man from the city. You sure you're not him?"

"No, ma'am. What are you meeting about?"

"We think they're dumping raw sewage here. We've had certain, uh, material wash up in the lagoon. The city denies it, so I'm meeting with an inspector to show him."

"You think it originated from here?"

Instead of answering him, she pushed forward. He followed and was treated to a history lesson of the wetlands and of the local environmentalists' ongoing battle with the Summa Corporation to restore the marshes.

Ignoring the NO TRESPASSING signs, they walked inland through a narrow path cut through stalks of wild licorice and Indian tobacco. The woman called out the various names of the plant life as they passed by.

At the Lincoln overpass, she paused and pointed downward. "Last month, we strung a net across the channel here," she explained. "We've been trying to crack down on dumping." She pointed to the buoys floating across the water. Mace noticed that she had cut her hand. A thin trickle of blood dripped out of a rent in the parchmentlike skin. He pulled a handkerchief from his pocket and blotted the blood as she explained how the net was weighted.

Mace reached down and pulled a stick out of his shoe; a large spider ran down his pants leg and he shook it off. Foxtails wove into his socks and pricked his ankles. He wished he wasn't wearing slacks.

He returned his attention to where the woman pointed. If the body parts had been dumped upriver, they would have been tangled in the net. That meant the arm had been dumped downriver from Lincoln. That still didn't account for the sand and vegetation. If the murderer(?) meant to bury the arm, how had it been transported over the six-foot berm bordering the Ballona Creek Channel? Did the guy think twice about burying his dismembered victim, dig a piece up, and toss it into the water? It would have been safer to leave the meat-laden bones to the feral dogs and turkey vultures that patrolled the marsh. After a day, nothing would have been left but scattered bones.

They climbed through an opening in the chain-link fence erected by the city to designate its claim on the property and walked along the four-foot-wide easement bordering the banks of the concrete-enclosed creek. The woman pointed to a great blue heron flying low over the water. The two of them paused to admire the bird's grace in flight, long legs trailing, neck curved delicately as it scanned the water for food. Spotting something, the bird dived; a sigh of appreciation escaped the two humans' lips. Mace could understand this woman's passion to preserve a habitat for these animals. The water rippled subtly, he noted with surprise, away from the ocean.

"Tide's coming in," the woman said, as if reading his thoughts.

At the Culver overpass, they again climbed through a hole in the fence, crossed the busy street, and then went back down into the wetlands. The land wasn't as flat nearer to the sea. Patches of sow thistle vied for space among the invasive pampas grass. Feathery white plumes nodded in the gentle breeze. The breeze also carried a medicinal scent from nearby eucalyptus trees. Mace noted that the pods were abloom, encouraged by the previous fortnight's downpour.

They came to the charred remains of an abandoned building. She explained that the concrete foundation and blackened timber were all that was left of the old UCLA crew house.

"Loyola Marymount University begged Howard Hughes for the use of the building after UCLA moved closer to the marina," she explained. "Hughes owned all this land. UCLA didn't want Loyola to get it. Burned down mysteriously a couple years back." She put a knowing finger to the side of her nose and fixed Mace with a look that said she had her own suspicions about the origins of that blaze.

Mace nodded and studied the site of the old crew house. The overgrown trees encircled what was now only a blackened collection of pilings. Dense overgrowth held fast wind-broken branches. The lifeless boughs hung there, dead and brown. Long slender leaves pointed downward and the silk from spent pod blossoms intertwined with the twiggy stems. The trunks of the trees were swathed in shabby robes of peeling bark. They made Mace think of ancient bearded Druids crowded around some smouldering campfire.

"We used to have a problem with transients camping out here," the woman said. "But why should they sleep outdoors when there are perfectly sound and conveniently abandoned homes just a few miles to the south?"

Mace looked to where she pointed, but all he could see were the red tile roofs and whitewashed walls of the Spanish-style buildings that marked the northernmost point of Loyola Marymount University. The chapel's delicate steeple was silhouetted against the hazy morning sky high on the Westchester bluffs. White rocks spelled out the letters LMU on the hillside.

The woman was referring to the ghost town on the other side of the bluffs. The formerly thriving suburb of Palisades del Rey, a collection of single-family dwellings with ocean views. The Free Zone was the area's official name, an innocent-sounding euphemism for what amounted to the forced eviction of an entire community.

Mace nodded. "I use to work with a guy whose family had a house there. They held out and fought the city's claim of eminent domain."

"They were smart, then," she said. "The people who sold at the first price the city offered didn't do so well. Have you been up there lately? It's eerie. Paved streets leading nowhere. A few of the homes are still there, waiting to be moved to somewhere else, somewhere other than the flight path of the jumbo jets."

"The guy I worked with had some high-placed friends in the city government," Mace said.

"That always helps."

Mace learned that the wetlands of Ballona, until just recently, were wetlands in name only. Deprived of the water that had once seeped out to nourish the marsh, the teeming ecosystem had been laid to waste. The wetlands were just now starting to come back. It was thanks to the leaking flap gates, she explained, that separated creek and marsh.

Mace pointed to a plant that he recognized as being the same as what he had recovered from the arm.

"We call it pickle weed," she said, glancing casually at the gray-green succulent leaves. "Grows pretty much exclusively in the marsh here to the south of the river. You'll also find some up in the Malibu dunes."

"And this?" he asked, pulling a prickly pod from a bush.

"Castor bean. It's poisonous, you know."

He didn't think the victim had died of poison. He shook his head and allowed himself a wry smile.

She pushed past him, intent on the ground. "Aha!" she said, spotting something. She bent down and scooped up a handful of sandy dirt. "You see this?" From the handful of earth in her hand, she plucked a pinch of sprouts and rubbed them between her fingers. She sniffed at the ground-up plants, then gestured for Mace to do the same. The plant had a familiar bite to it.

"What is that?" he asked.

"Tomato plants." She stared at him as if he was the dumbest person ever to cross her path. "How the hell you think these got here? Sure sign of raw sewage. Don't they teach you fellas anything?"

Behind the woman, a green Chevrolet with a city seal on the passenger door pulled up to the curb. She turned when she heard the car door open.

"There he is," the woman said. "Let's see him deny it now." She put two fingers to her mouth and whistled shrilly in the direction of the fat inspector getting out of his car. The dog at her heels raised his head and waved his tail feebly. They waited while the man waddled to where they stood, using his clipboard to help him balance.

"We have proof," the woman proclaimed. She shoved her damning evidence under the inspector's nose.

The inspector smoothed down his tie and straightened the plastic name tag clipped importantly to his lapel. He looked down at his clipboard, then pointed at Mace. "Who's this?"

Mace flipped open the leather case that held his badge. "Police." He winked at the woman. "Answer the lady."

"We've given your complaint serious attention." The man consulted his clipboard. "On the evening of January thirtieth, engineers at the Hyperion water-treatment plant recorded an incident. We had heavy rains that evening, if you remember. A quarter inch had been predicted."

"I remember that night," the woman said. "It rained for hours. We were watching *Roots;* it was part seven."

"That was part of the incident." The man made a deliberate show of fingering his official badge and hitching his pants before he found his place on his paperwork and continued, obviously relishing his man-with-the-clipboard moment. "Fifty-one percent of the viewing public was also watching. At the first commercial, so many toilets flushed simultaneously throughout the city that water pressure dropped to almost nothing for six minutes."

Mace nodded; he'd read about that.

"What goes down," the inspector continued, "must come out. The engineers at Hyperion, who had been monitoring the already-brimming sewers all evening, were forced to take emergency action. There was no way the facility could handle the resulting flood of waste water. They were forced to open the emergency floodgates at the Culver Boulevard pumping station."

"I knew it," the woman said, patting her dog on his bony head. "We were right."

The inspector rolled his eyes.

37

"I've been instructed to assure you that it won't happen again."
He busied himself by marking something off on his paperwork.
No doubt to be filed in triplicate somewhere, Mace thought.

Mace excused himself and walked back to study the banks running along the marsh side of the creek. Three feet up the bank,
he found a residue of scum: tiny balls of Styrofoam, traces of salt,
a thin layer of sand that came away easily when he brushed his
hand across the concrete. He returned to his car and drove to the
Coast Guard station. There, he studied tidal charts. On the
evening of the thirtieth, he learned, between the hours of 6:39
and 11:06 P.M., low tide dipped to minus one and half feet. Ex-
cited now, he returned to the flap gates and shined his flashlight
into the culvert beneath the easement. He called the department
from a pay phone and spoke with the watch commander.

"I think I've figured out how the arm from the Ballona Creek
victim ended up where it did," he told the duty officer. "I'm going
to need a diving team."

The divers met Mace at the flap gates downstream from the
UCLA crew house. The flap gates had swung open when the level
of water in the creek dropped below the flooded level of the wetlands, releasing God knows what all into the ocean. The arm must
have been carried upstream by the returning tide, Mace deduced.
If they were lucky, maybe the team would recover a head and,
more important, a mouth full of teeth. Twenty minutes later, the
divers surfaced with a grim find—two decomposed human legs,
flecks of red polish still visible on the toenails. That was all, no
head.

Mace called Carol and asked her to meet him at the coroner's
office. By noon, they were huddled over the rotting limbs.

From the length of the bones and degree of muscle and fat,
Carol was able to estimate stature. She explained to him that by
the age of twenty-five, thighbones and shinbones reach the stage
of maximum development—known as ossification; the bones
harden into their final length. She checked the soft tissue of the

bone for hardening and found it still soft, putting the girl's age at somewhere in her late teens or early twenties. They made casts of the feet and of the whole legs and reconstructed their original shapes from estimations of water absorption. The culvert was drained, but nothing more was found that was pertinent to the case. A skull was recovered, obviously canine.

Carol and he spent the rest of the afternoon going over every inch of the body parts.

"At least they're a matched set, a left and a right," she said, showing Mace that she could be an optimist. Then they got lucky. X rays revealed a bullet from a .22 lodged in the muscle of one of the quadriceps and perfectly preserved. They photographed the ballistic fingerprints of the bullet and added this new evidence to the file.

Unfortunately, there wasn't much else. They were unable to find the bullet's entry wound. No doubt the surrounding charred skin left from the heat of the bullet had disintegrated quickly in the shallow salt water. Carol found spots of motor oil on the right calf in what appeared to be a spray pattern. They then addressed the question of how the legs and arm had been severed from the torso. They discovered ligature marks left by a heavy chain. The reddish links of bruises on the wrist and in similar indentations on the skin of the ankles indicated that the bruising had occurred while the victim was alive. Carol measured the width and length of the links with a micrometer. She announced that two different chains appeared to have been used.

That night, Mace bought a whole chicken and took it to his father's house. Wrapping thin chains around the tips of the bird's legs and wings, he attempted to pull the bird apart over the double sink in the kitchen. Digger watched from a chair with mild curiosity.

"Wouldn't it be easier if you cooked it first?" he finally asked.

"No, it has to be raw." Mace answered. "But you've got a good point." He grabbed a cleaver and hacked at the joints. The legs pulled apart from the carcass, still tearing flesh and muscle in mimicry of his partial corpse. "Good thinking. Thanks."

Digger smiled and asked, "You gonna make potatoes, too?"

Mace couldn't wait to tell everyone how Digger had come through for him.

5

Munch spent Sunday huddled in her car. Traffic was light. She couldn't stop yawning in between the shaking and sweating. She wondered if they were looking for her. Her bones ached. She smoked and waited.

At midday, she got out and stretched. The oleanders provided a thick screen from the street. She opened the trunk of the car and found an old army blanket, which she wrapped around her shoulders. She'd read once that oleander was poisonous, and now she wondered briefly how many leaves she would have to chew. With her luck, she'd just get more sick, if that was possible. She returned to the cave of her backseat and huddled in the blanket.

By four o'clock on Monday morning, she decided it was a bad hour to be awake, no matter where you were. The night is at its darkest and coldest. It's a lonely hour, not that you would want to meet anyone else out and about. She watched the clock on the dashboard rotate. Occasionally, she felt the rumble of the ground as a big truck passed. At 5:15, the sky began to lighten. By six o'clock, lights were coming on in the homes around her. The boulevard began to hum as the residents went about their daily business. She was out of cigarettes.

She ran her fingers through her hair and over her clothes. The green knit top she had grabbed in Saturday night's flight fit reasonably well and almost matched the paisley jeans she had snatched. She wished she'd taken the time to grab some socks.

She crossed the road and tried to get her bearings. She saw a car approaching and looked down. Then she realized she was being ridiculous. She doubted very much that her picture had made the evening news or the morning papers. Guys were getting killed all the time, all over the city, and you never heard about it unless it was some rich guy or something. Flower George hardly qualified. God, was he really dead? She could barely believe it, but she had been there, so she knew.

She looked ahead of her, farther up the road, no sense in looking back. In the distance, a yellow Denny's sign glowed. She stumbled down the shoulder of the boulevard under cover of the bushes and tall weeds. She wasn't sure where she was, but they probably wouldn't think to look for her here. In the Denny's bathroom, she washed her face and counted her money. It was still only fourteen dollars.

Cigarettes, she needed cigarettes.

She rolled up the cuffs of the pants and tucked in the shirt before she went back out into the restaurant.

The cashier made change for her. Munch put her quarters in the machine and pulled the knob under the Pall Malls. When she lit a match, the smell of sulphur made her stomach grip in anticipation. The monster was calling.

"Gonna have breakfast, honey?" The waitress was too cheerful in her pink dress and sensible white shoes. Her smile was sincere enough; it just hurt the eyes. A name tag over her right breast read HI, I'M RUBY.

Munch counted the change in her hand. "No. I ain't having nothing."

"Let me give you a cup of coffee."

"Why would you do that?"

"You look like you could use a little help."

"I'll have a cup, black. But I'll pay for it." She wondered if the waitress was a lesbo or something.

"Here you go." Ruby slid a stack of buttered toast and jam in front of her. "The last guy didn't want his order of toast. I'd already made it. Shame for it to go to waste, don't you think?" Munch shrugged and eyed the woman warily. When Ruby went to the back to get an order, Munch took a bite. The hot food opened the floodgates of her salivary glands. The buttered toast was even better with strawberry jam. This was the way she imagined food would taste in the country, fresh off the farm. She ate the whole plateful.

The waitress returned to refill her coffee.

"Thanks."

"You're welcome, hon."

Munch drank the second cup, left a thirty-five-cent tip, and pocketed the remaining packets of jam. When the waitress was busy with another customer, she left. The Denny's was on a busy intersection; cars rode one another's bumpers six deep in every direction. She stepped out into the street and sized up the neighborhood. It was mostly businesses: a car wash, locksmith, an Italian deli. Across the street was an auto shop identified by a faded wooden sign lit with a solitary spotlight. Happy Jack's Auto Repair appeared to be open. The doors of the lube bay were raised and a mechanic labored under the hood of a large sedan. In the office window, a red-and-white sign propped up with a vase of daisies read NOW HIRING. She crossed the street and tried to ignore the cramps in her stomach.

The office of Happy Jack's Auto Repair was a permanently anchored trailer set on cinder blocks. Three wooden steps led to a front door made of galvanized steel, which looked as if it had been kicked in once or twice. Filing cabinets and posters advertising Gabriel shock absorber specials filled the back wall.

The door was open and there was a man inside speaking on the phone. He was fiftyish and heavyset. She climbed the stairs and rapped lightly on the door. The man acknowledged her pres-

43

ence with a raised index finger, then swiveled around till he faced the back wall, leaving her to study the bald spot on the back of his head. His tone was consoling and he repeatedly rubbed his temples with a calloused hand as he spoke to his caller. She sat on a bench under the window and leafed through a *Road & Track* magazine till he finished his call.

He hung up the phone with a bang and turned to face her. She spoke first.

"You looking for a mechanic?"

She felt the man size her up. She tried not to flinch when he looked at the toes showing through the tops of her Keds.

"You know someone who's looking?"

"Me."

He started to smile. She stared him out of his dismissive grin.

"Look, kid, no offense, but I don't think you could handle it."

"Jack—" A skinny mechanic in coveralls burst in the office, then stopped in midsentence. "Oh, sorry, I didn't realize you were busy."

"What you need, Lou?"

"I can't figure out what's wrong with that Thunderbird we tuned last week. It got towed in last night. The note says it just quit on the guy."

"That was him on the phone. He's really pissed."

Munch stood. "If I get it running, can I have the job?"

Both men stared at her. Lou's eyes lingered on her shoes and she glared back at him.

"What have you got to lose?" She held out her hand. "I'll need a screwdriver."

Jack nodded. "Let her try." Lou shook his head and mumbled something under his breath.

They all walked out into the lot together. The hood of the Ford was up and the air cleaner rested on the ground. All Lou had been able to do was hook the car up to various life support. Cables from a battery charger and scope snaked out from the engine. She disconnected the scope and shut off the charger, the smell

44

of rotten eggs telling her that the battery was roasting inside. At the cab company, she had had a milk crate that she stood on. When she worked on bigger vehicles, she scrambled up the front and sat in the engine compartment. Now, she hoisted herself up on the fender and lay across it belly-down. She peered inside the carburetor. Her sneakered feet dangled a foot above the tarmac. "It's getting plenty of gas," Lou said when he saw her work the throttle.

She sniffed the opening of the carburetor and then stuck a finger inside and tasted the gas. Lou and Jack exchanged amused looks. "Turn the key on, will you?" she asked him.

"You want me to crank it?"

"Nah, I'll do it from the solenoid." She pulled out the coil wire and held it a quarter inch from the center tower of the distributor cap. She jumped the solenoid connections with the screwdriver. The spark coming out of the coil was erratic: blue, then yellow, then nonexistent, then blue again. The engine sputtered, backfired, tried to run, then died. She popped off the distributor cap, loosened the screw holding the ignition condenser, and carefully pried loose the small silver cylinder. "Got a lighter?"

"You gonna have a cigarette?" Jack asked, looking more baffled than happy.

Lou handed her his Zippo. She held the flame under the lead wire of the condenser. The insulation melted away. "Watch," she said, and the terminal end of the wire dropped off. "You had a break in the wire inside of the insulation."

"That was a brand-new condenser," Lou said. "It was right off the shelf, Jack. You handed it to me yourself. How was I supposed to know?"

"There was a service bulletin on this last month." She looked at the two men. "Do I have the job?"

"Sure, kid. What's your name?"

She looked past his shoulder to the window of the office. "Daisy."

"Daisy what?"

"Daisy . . . Sign . . . man."

"Okay, Miss Daisy Signman, let's see if we got a set of coveralls that'll fit you."

Lou set his mouth. "She just got lucky."

"Why don't you read those service bulletins?"

Lou glared at her.

WHEN Mace got to work Monday morning, he received thumbs-up from the other detectives of the morning shift. They all congratulated him on the keen detective work that resulted in the discovery of the legs. Mace acknowledged their praise but was worried about command's reaction. Captain Divine was sure to be upset at what he would perceive as an undermining of his authority.

On the way to the morning briefing, Mace spotted a group of visiting dignitaries walking down the hallway with the captain. There were several elected officials from City Hall, and a congressman with them. Mace held his breath as the senior officers approached. The congressman stretched out his hand. "Good work, son."

Divine picked up his cue. "Well done, Detective."

Mace wondered if this would be a good time to bring up the issue of overtime.

The morning briefing was mercifully short. Accounts were given of ongoing investigations. Mace delivered a brief report on the weekend homicides. At the close of the meeting, Divine asked if there were any grievances. The detectives stayed wisely mute.

As far as the Ballona Butcher case was concerned, it was agreed that all the detectives could do now was wait hopefully for a lead, a phone call, some tip. The fingerprints taken from the arm had already been checked against known records, but no matches had been found.

Someone put a hand-drawn portrait on the station's bulletin board. A legless woman with one sleeve knotted at the shoulder and the caption "Have you seen me?"

When Mace returned to his desk, the results of the Flower George lab work were waiting for him. The prints on the van and the glass had been a match. No-brainer there, he thought. The girl had been ID'd at the house by Vice and seen driving the van. The computer delivered a name and picture to go with the prints. Miranda Blowme was one of the names she had given when she was booked. *Cute.* In the picture, her thin lips compressed in an angry line. Mousy light brown hair spilled out of a short ponytail secured with a rubber band. One eye was blackened. In the darkness of the bar, he hadn't been able to determine the shade of her large eyes, only that they were set in a tiny face and underscored with dark gashes. The mug shot was in black and white. A written description listed her eyes as "hazel." Her face reminded him of the camp art that had surfaced in the early sixties. She looked like one of that artist Keane's big-eyed waifs with the oval faces and long necks. He pinned the picture to the bulletin board behind his desk. She'd probably turned a trick on her way home from jail. That's how those whores were. It was stupid to waste man power busting them.

He dialed the switchboard and asked them to call the Santa Monica Probation Department. The officer assigned to his suspect was Caroline Rhinehart. That right there was reason enough for a follow-up. He'd been drooling over Miss Caroline Rhinehart since the first time he'd seen her cross her slender legs. There was something so orderly about her, pure class. She wore her blond hair shoulder length and he liked the way it flipped outward at the bottom. Her makeup was subdued, not overdone. She didn't paint her lids blue to bring out her eyes or overdo it with the eyeliner and mascara till she looked like Elizabeth Taylor's Cleopatra. Her whole attitude seemed to say, This is who I am and it's damn good enough. There was a competence about her that he appreciated. She'd been labeled a cold bitch by the other cops, who misread her dedication. He'd immediately seen beyond her aloofness. She had a reputation for being tough but fair with her clients. She'd give anyone the benefit of the doubt, he'd heard, but she was also a realist. In this business, you had to be. It had taken him a marriage to catch on, but he'd learned.

She said she didn't date cops. He hadn't been able to get a fix on the kind of guy she did go for. Probably some touchy-feely kind of wimp who cried at sad movies.

Maybe she wanted a talker, like his ex had. "What's to talk about?" he'd asked his wife when she voiced her unhappiness. "There's them and us," he told her. She hadn't been interested in his "negative philosophies." They'd tried counseling. What a joke that had been. Waste of money. The big fight that drove them there had been just as stupid. She wanted to go to midnight Mass and he told her absolutely not. He had just spent the previous forty-eight hours investigating a double homicide. Two women out at night alone. Did she want to talk about the damage done to a woman's chest by a couple of double-aught shells fired at close range by some asshole in need of gas money? He wasn't about to burden her with that disturbing image. He told her she would just have to trust him on this one. She told the shrink that he was interfering with her right to worship God. He said she could worship God till her heart's content at the morning Mass. The psychiatrist suggested a Minnesota Multiphasic Personality Inventory. Among other things, the doctor said the test measured Mace's degree of protectiveness. He scored a 98 percent. What more did she want? In the car on the way home, she told him that the good doctor said a normal score was from 30 to 70 percent. Like the asshole had any idea what "normal" meant. Then she had asked him to move out, but he still paid half the bills. How did his buddy, Bob, put it? "The fucking he was getting for the fucking he got." It would have been simpler just to pay for it straight out.

When Mace told his then partner, Ernie Potts, about the results of the test, Ernie had been incredulous. "You ever take that test again," he said, "you come see me first. Nobody can pass that test who's been a cop for any length of time. You gotta know how to answer those questions. Next time, talk to me first; you'll ace that test."

The switchboard patched him through to Caroline Rhinehart's office.

"Ms. Rhinehart? Mace St. John here with the Venice PD."

"What can I do for you, Detective?"

"Well, it's a rather complicated matter involving one of your clients. I really think it would be best if we met in person to discuss this. How about lunch?" The furthest he'd ever gotten with her was a shared cup of coffee from the vending machine.

"I have a previous engagement. Does this so-called client have a name?"

"Blowme, Miranda."

"I beg your pardon?"

"Hey, you asked."

"Oh, you mean Munch. What's she done?"

"It's looking like murder one."

"Oh God. I'm really sorry to hear that." He heard her sigh and he wished he hadn't been so flip. "Who's she accused of murdering?"

"Some low-life pimp named George Mancini. Street name: Flower George."

"That poor kid." She sighed again. He wondered if she was crossing her legs and if she was wearing that beige suit with the skirt that hiked up her thigh. "I know the name. Flower George was her father."

A little twist went off somewhere in Mace's intestine like the tightening of a knot. "We're not looking for her that hard."

"Do me a favor."

"Anything." He wasn't thinking about her legs anymore. He

was thinking about a scrawny little throwaway complaining that sex with her pimp old man took too long. He felt queasy.

"Let me know if anything more comes up."

"I'll be in court most of the day. In fact, I'll be right by your office. If we get out early enough, would it be all right if I stopped by and looked at the girl's file?"

"I'll wait for you," she said.

6

At noon on Monday, the shop broke for lunch. Munch used the time to go to the bathroom, where she gave herself a sponge bath with her bandanna and the cold tap water. The stomach cramps were much worse. The pain centered around her belly button and radiated outward till it reached the insides of her arms. A spike stabbed between her legs. Every cell in her body craved relief. Just a taste, the voice said.

When she came out of the bathroom, Jack and Lou were sitting together on the low block wall at the front of the shop. They were eating sandwiches and drinking coffee out of white ceramic mugs smudged with greasy fingerprints.

"Come join us," Jack called out. "You can help us decide a very important matter: what kind of flowers to plant." He pointed to the squares of brown earth beneath his feet and an empty bed around the base of a pine tree that grew incongruously in the center of the lot.

"Why'd you plant a tree there?" she had to ask.

"I didn't." He swallowed and waved toward the tree with his sandwich. "The damn thing pushed right through the asphalt. I was planning to pull it; in fact, I did once. Damn thing grew right back. I was going to pour gas on the sapling, kill the roots, and then fill in the hole. Then I figured anything that worked that hard to survive deserved a chance. So I broke up the asphalt around it and made another flower bed."

"It looks nice." She nodded to the empty office. "I need to make some phone calls. Is that all right?"

"As long as they're local." He resumed his discussion with Lou. She heard him say something about petunias as she climbed the steps to the office. Her legs felt like they were made of cement. Fresh sweat broke out on her forehead as another stomach cramp almost made her double over.

She sat at the desk and pulled open a local phone book. She pulled the handful of assorted little containers of jams and jellies that she had liberated from the Denny's out of her shirt pocket. While she searched, she peeled open a little box of marmalade and licked it clean. She found what she was after on the third call.

"St. Anthony's," a woman answered.

"I need to get baptized. Do you do that?"

There was a pause on the line while the woman considered. "Yes, we do. Babies, usually. Would you like a meeting with Father Frank?"

"As soon as possible. I don't have much time."

"All right, dear. It sounds very important to you. How about this afternoon?"

"How much does it cost?"

"It's customary to make a donation."

"I don't have much money, either."

"Just bring your faith, dear. I'm sure everything will work out."

"You'll give me a certificate and everything, right?" Happy Jack had finished his lunch and was walking toward the office. The woman assured her that they would.

She got directions and swept the jam wrappers into the wastebasket next to the desk.

A shadow fell across the desk as Jack's big torso filled the office door. "I need you to fill out a W-four while I got you in here."

He fished in the file cabinet till he found what he was after and then handed her the form. "I need your Social Security number, address, and I'm going to need a copy of your driver's license for our insurance."

"It's gonna take me a couple of days to get all my stuff. I gotta go somewhere at four." She challenged him with her eyes to say no. If he did, fuck him—she didn't care. She was looking for a job when she found this one. He just looked back at her as if she'd hurt his feelings. For some reason, that made her feel bad. "It won't take long." She tried to make her mouth smile.

"All right, we'll see you first thing in the morning." He picked up the application she had begun to fill out. "That's good you live so close. You can finish filling this out later. I see you left the 'next of kin' and 'whom to notify in case of an emergency' lines blank."

"What kind of emergency?"

"If you get hurt or something."

"I'll have to think about that," she said.

She tore out the page in the phone book that listed community services and stuck it in her pocket. The Social Security office was only two blocks away. She knew from recent experience that all she had to do was tell them that she'd never had a card before and they'd type one up for her on the spot.

"I can work till three-thirty. By the way, when do I get paid?"

Happy Jack gave her an amused look. "Friday. You a little short?" He smiled at his own pun.

"I'll get by."

"You remind me of my wife's Chihuahua, Missy. Nine pounds of pure terror." He chuckled. "She's a feisty little thing. She's bitten me twice, thinks I'm trying to hurt my wife when I hug her. The little mutt thinks she's a Doberman. Dog's got heart all right."

"Why don't you just kick her or something?"

"Nah, why? She's got the right idea. She's just being loyal. I can't punish her for that. Ever had a dog, Daisy?"

"I never wanted one." She poked at the desk leg with the toe of her tennis shoe. "They just die."

Lou walked through the door. "Daisy," he said, and looked from the flowers by the window to her. "That sounds like something you'd name a dog. Is that a nickname you picked up? I don't see how." He spit out the door. "Sure isn't very much flowerlike about you."

"She's got a way with an engine; you gotta give her that," Jack said. He put a hand on her shoulder. "She's one of those natural-born mechanics, woman or no. She's got the ear for it." He patted her back and said, "We're gonna have to get you some small coveralls. Those mediums make you look like a little kid."

After the girl left the office, Happy Jack started clearing his desk—writing bills, and totaling work orders. He tore off an invoice carbon, balled it in his meaty hand, but he paused before he threw it away. The empty tubs of jam on top of the trash caused him to hesitate.

Daisy was already back at work, jacking up the front end of a Chevrolet. The two men watched her stand on the lug wrench and use the weight of her body to loosen the lug nuts, like she was kick-starting a motorcycle.

"Smart." Jack put his big palm over his mouth and massaged his jaw. "Better to work smart. See, a woman has to use her brain more. She can't just bull it through with brute strength."

Lou turned to his boss. "What the hell did you hire her for? Just because she got lucky with that Ford?"

"You got a problem working with a woman, Lou?" He raised a brow at his employee.

"All I'm trying to tell you is that a woman isn't built for this kind of work; she's got no future here. This is crazy. She's taking a job from a man, maybe some man with a family to support." Lou glanced down at Jack's desk. He picked up the photograph there and showed it to Jack. "She reminds you of your sister, doesn't she?"

"Maybe. Listen, we'll give her a couple of weeks and see how she does. If she can't cut it, she's out of here."

THE Probation Department where Munch Mancini had been assigned was on the first floor of the Santa Monica courthouse. Caroline Rhinehart's office was a three-sided cubicle. She stood when Mace announced himself by rapping lightly on the jamb of her open doorway.

"Come in, Sergeant. Have a seat." Her desk faced one wall, so that when Mace sat in the chair reserved for her clients, she sat opposite him, with no furniture to obstruct his view. She handed him a file and her fingers briefly brushed his wrist. He could tell a lot about a woman by the way she kept her hands. Caroline's were clean and soft, her nails evenly tapered and painted a delicate shade of pink that matched her lipstick.

"This is Munch's file."

He scanned the report. It said, "Miranda Blowme, aka Munch Mancini, last arrested November 11, 1976. Charges: 647B, prostitution; 11721 H&S, possession of a controlled substance; 4149 B&P, narcotic paraphernalia; CBC 148.9, supplying a police officer with false information. Served twenty-three days at Sybil Brand Institute for Women. Sentenced to twenty-three days (time served), one year suspended, and two years probation."

"Whenever I get a new client, I give them a writing assignment." She put a sheet of notebook paper on top of the file on his lap. "I ask them to write down what their dream life would be like. I don't put any limits on their fantasy. I tell them just to write the perfect life for themselves. This was Munch's response."

He read the block printing.

"My perfect life," Munch had written, "would be if I could live in the country. I would have a house that only I lived in. I would own my own Harley, which I would ride to work each day. I would work at the gas station in town."

That was it. He turned the paper over in his hand. The back was blank.

"How would you have answered the question, Miss Rhinehart?"

She thought a moment. "In my perfect life," she said finally, "my job wouldn't be necessary. How about you?"

"My job will always be necessary."

She put her hand on his and leaned toward him. Her wide-spaced eyes were intense as she stared into his. They were like the sky, a sky full of clouds that kept changing. He could get lost in eyes like hers, if he allowed himself. "You could make a difference here. Help this girl; she's never had a break."

It was difficult, but he pulled his hand away from hers. "I'm not a social worker," he said. "I'm a homicide detective. If a murder is committed, it has to be answered for."

"Isn't there such a thing as justifiable homicide?"

"That's not for me to decide. You know that. Is there something more about this case that I should know?"

She gave him another searching look. He found he couldn't maintain eye contact, so he looked away. "No," she answered after a minute. "Nothing concrete, just a feeling."

His hand was still warm where she had grabbed it. He wanted to tell her that he knew what she meant, but that was silly. She wasn't even sure of what she felt. "Just get her to come in and talk," he said, "if she contacts you."

"She won't. She thinks I have it in for her. She doesn't trust women."

Who does? Mace thought, but instead he asked, "What does she think of men?"

"They are definitely the enemy."

"Doesn't leave anybody else, does it?"

She just shook her head and bored into him with those stormy blue eyes of hers.

AT four o'clock, Munch changed back into her street clothes and took off walking. St. Anthony's Episcopal Church was four blocks away and her appointment with the priest was set for 4:15. Their ad in the Yellow Pages said they were a "progressive" church. Her stomach cramps were more persistent now. She alternated between chills and sweats.

St. Anthony's grounds took up half a city block. The church

itself was an elaborate structure with an ornate facade that was adorned with grape vines chiseled in stone. Above the front door, a crucified Christ looked down benevolently. She shivered at the sight of the nails driven through his feet and hands and scratched her arms in sympathy. Weird religion. Near the sidewalk, there was a directory mounted in a glass case with a map of the buildings. She studied it; her finger rested on the red arrow that informed "You are here." The lady on the phone had said that Father Frank would meet with her in the rectory. Munch had said she hoped it wouldn't take all day. The lady said it would take what it took—they were on God's time.

Wooden signposts directed her across a large courtyard filled with a well-tended rose garden, bird baths, and several wooden benches. She came to a large oak door with a brass nameplate that identified the room as Fellowship Hall. On the other side of the door people were laughing and talking. The door swung open and she saw a plate of doughnuts set out on a folding table next to a stack of Styrofoam cups. She wasn't sure what force drew her more, the doughnuts or the laughter. The clock on the wall said it was ten after four. She stepped inside.

"Welcome!" a woman shouted in her face. "Are you new?"

"Maybe."

"Come in. There's literature on the credenza. Help yourself to refreshments."

She didn't know what the hell a credenza was, but refreshments were clear enough. She grabbed three doughnuts, sticking two under her shirt. The greeter at the door swooped down on her with two more church ladies in tow. She cringed as the woman lowered her arms around her shoulders. "What's your name, honey?"

"Daisy Signman."

"We just use first names here, dear. Is this your first meeting?"

"I'm here to see Father Frank. He's going to baptize me. In fact, I'm going to be late." She twisted out from under the woman's arms. Was this whole town full of lesbos, or what? She didn't go in for that shit. She half-ran out the door and followed the signs pointing to the rectory, cramming the doughnuts down as fast as she could.

The man waiting for her there, who introduced himself as Father Frank, wasn't what she had expected. He wasn't wearing long black robes and wasn't a hundred years old. In place of the clerical garb were jeans. His only concession to convention was a black shirt with one of those funny white collars. She wiped her palms on her pants before she accepted his soft, warm hand and welcoming smile.

"How can I help you?"

To her horror, she felt her lip begin to quiver. She wasn't ready for this. She had expected judgment, distrust, the wariness that she always brought out in people—the same wariness she brought with her to all her dealings. This was the point where the barter should begin. There was always some kind of trade involved. The idea was to give as little as possible to get as much as possible. No one ever began by asking what they could do for her. She felt tears forming behind her eyes and blinked them back.

"I don't have much money. I told the lady on the phone."

"Mrs. Waters tells me that you said your time was also limited." Father Frank gestured for her to sit. "We've decided to waive charges, if you're sincere in your desire to make peace with the Lord."

There, she knew there would be a catch. He wanted her to say she believed in all his mumbo jumbo. "What do I have to do?"

"I have selected a passage—from the Twenty-third Psalm— that has always been a special comfort to me. Please, come pray with me."

"What if I don't know the words?"

"You can read along." He handed her a small black book with a cross embossed on its leather cover. He opened it to a page he had marked with a ribbon. "We'll start here."

She took the book from him and started to read. " 'Yeah, thought I travel through the valley—' "

"That's 'Yea.' " he interrupted. " 'Yea, *though* I travel *through* the valley.' "

She looked up at him and nodded once, then began again, " 'Yea, though I travel through the valley of the shadow of death, I shall fear no evil.' " Her eyes began to blur and from somewhere deep within her, someplace she had closed off, she felt a stirring, an opening of a door. The tears came then, the ones that had been held at bay but had never dried up. A flood followed that choked her voice and streaked her face.

Father Frank nodded. He didn't stop reciting till the passage was finished. Then he led her to a stone bowl in the chapel garden under a statue of the Madonna and her child. He dipped his fingers in the bowl and made the sign of the cross on her forehead. When the ceremony was concluded, he gave her a baptismal certificate, embossed with the church's seal. She tried to give him the Bible back, but he stopped her.

"That's for you. Study it. Come back."

She folded the document carefully and stuck it in the cover of the book. He had written something on the first page. "For Daisy," it said in neat cursive. "When God is with you, who can be against you? Sincerely, Father Franklin Bartlett."

"Thank you, Father. You don't know how much this means to me." She left the church and headed toward Van Nuys Boulevard for the Department of Motor Vehicles, which viewed a certificate of baptism as equal to a birth certificate as proof of birth. The priest wanted sincerity, and he got it. She tried to smirk but gave up. It was too hard to do with a quivering chin. Who was she trying to kid? Deep down, she knew she wasn't that good an actress, and now all that deep-down stuff seemed to be right on the surface.

7

_____

Before Mace returned to the Bella Donna, he stopped at the gym to shower and shave. But first, he slipped on a pair of training gloves and punched halfheartedly at the uppercut bag, gradually building into a rhythm. Above the bag hung a homemade sign that said, NO SMOKEING. Mace hadn't had the heart to correct the kid who'd made the mistake on the sign. Besides, he'd made his point, and that was what mattered.

On the far wall, Hector "Romeo" Sanchez's picture grinned down at him from the display case. Hector's rippled torso was adorned with the wide golden belt of a champion. Mace raised his glove in acknowledgment of the boy's achievement. Hector was the exception. He'd come to the gym and hooked up with Digger before he had reached the point of no return. Instead of joining a gang, Hector wandered into the Vernon Street Gym and channeled all that hungry energy into something that could get him out of this pisshole.

The picture was old, but the display case was new, another donation by the Venice Police Department. The division had also donated the man power to build a second ring and add on to the locker room. Small bronze plaques affixed to the brick walls credited local lumber and hardware businesses with donations of materials. What the plaques didn't mention was the duress applied by one Officer Mace St. John, who offered to not make arrests for those business's use of illegal immigrants in return for their charitable, tax-deductible contributions.

"Stayin' Alive" came on the radio and someone turned the volume up.

"The fear will keep you pure" was scrawled on the wall behind the row of speed bags. The fear of being hurt in the ring kept the fighters training, sparring and jumping rope, on those days when they would rather just stretch out and watch a game. Mace had learned all about redirecting emotion in the army. Then, it was anger. In the jungle, the rage kept you numb. He had used his anger to get him through each day.

The bell rang, signaling the end of a three-minute round and beginning of the one-minute rest period. He began to punch the bag in earnest. It danced a hurky-jerky under the punishment of blows. Next, he went to the speed bag and got into a rhythm. The bag became a blur and drowned out the music around him and the hum of exhaust fans running at full tilt. The sweat poured down his body and stung his eyes.

There were no tough guys in the Vernon Street Gym. They left all that behind them the first time they stepped on the canvas or else they didn't make it. The trick was to weed out the individual from the gang. His wife had asked him once what the acronym CRIP stood for. "Cowards run in packs," he'd said. Pretty easy to be a tough guy when you had twenty homeboys to back you up. He liked to get that kind alone.

THE house Mace grew up in and Digger still lived in was on Carroll Canal. Carroll hadn't been a canal since the early part of the century, when the health department ordered the nonfunctioning waterways near the ocean filled in. Narrow streets of asphalt entombed the area between the rows of houses and duplexes where the water had once flowed too slowly. Digger's brown stucco one-story home with the cream-colored gingerbread trim had been built during the building boom at the end of World War II, one of the thousands built to accommodate all the soldiers returning from the war overseas who had decided they preferred the mild climate of California.

Digger moved his family there in 1946, when Mace was four. Now Evangeline, the ever-patient Filipina Mace had found to look after Digger, stayed in Mace's childhood room.

Mace parked in the alley behind the house and entered through the back door, which was unlocked, as usual. He'd told them both a hundred times to keep it dead-bolted, but they never did.

"Hello," he called out loudly, so they would hear him over the noise of the television. He stopped in the kitchen, opened the refrigerator, and riffled through various Tupperware containers stored neatly on the shelves. The first container yielded tuna fish salad. He grabbed a fork out of the drawer, tried a few bites, chased them down with a few swigs of milk, then moved on. Evangeline always kept fresh cut-up fruit on hand. Today's selection was a combination of papaya and cantaloupe. He speared a few wedges and popped them in his mouth. "You ready?" he yelled in the direction of the den. "I'm starving." The volume of the television turned down a notch.

"Ready for what?" Digger yelled back.

"Monday night—ribs, remember?" The doctors said that consistency would be good for Digger. Mace walked into the den.

"Of course I remember. What do you mean? You think I don't know?" Digger clicked off the television and scowled at his son.

"You're not wearing that? Where are those new slacks I bought you?" Mace turned to Evangeline, who only shrugged helplessly.

"I tried to tell him, Mr. Mace," she said. "He no listen. He do it his way."

"Dad, we're not going out with you dressed like that. You got on a yellow shirt and red pants. Why don't you wear that blue pinstripe and the cords I brought you?" He held out his hands and pulled Digger to his feet. Digger groaned with the effort. "Come in the bedroom; I'll help you."

"Okay, okay," the old man muttered. His once–dark brown hair had turned a silvery blond with the passage of years and had thinned to the point of transparency. In defiance of gravity, he grew the remaining strands long on one side and combed them over the top. As he rose grudgingly to his feet, the gossamer strands lifted straight up, then settled over his left ear, resting just short of his frayed collar. Mace smoothed the stray locks back in place and Digger mirrored the gesture with his own big hand. In his prime, Digger had been strong, quick, light on his feet, with hands so tough, they could put out cigars—the same big hands that had pummeled opponents in warm-up bouts at the Olympic Auditorium before the main event, ironed Mace's shirts for Sunday school, and whipped up a weekly treat of French toast after church. The tradition had begun when Mace was eight. It was a big year of change for both of them. That was the year Mace had been granted the honor of calling his dad by his nickname, "Digger." A reward for making the transition to "big boy," specifically one who didn't cry at his own mother's funeral. That was the year Digger had made the transition to trainer. In later years, Digger picked up extra cash sparring with the greats—Patterson, Marciano, Sugar Ray, Sonny Liston—maybe a few times too many.

Mace grabbed a tissue from the table by the armchair and wiped the moisture running from Digger's nose. His dad looked up at him.

"By the way, where are we going?"

"It's Monday night. We always get ribs on Monday night."

"That's right."

Half an hour later, they were in the car on their way to dinner. On the way out the door, Mace instructed Evangeline to throw out the red pants with the cigarette burns in them and to lock the door. When they came to the signal at Washington and Pacific, Digger turned to his son. "Where are we going?" he asked.

"It's a surprise, Dad."

"Oh," Digger said, and settled comfortably into his seat.

THE following day, Mace got to work early. Sitting on top of his desk were the threads of an investigation that had been left dangling since Friday. They called to him now, two small plastic evidence bags sitting on top of the clutter on his desk. One bag held the butt of a Viceroy cigarette, the other a burned match. The two bags represented the only physical evidence recovered from the scene of a brutal robbery/murder at the Glenwood Garden Apartments. The apartment complex sat right on the border of Marina del Rey and Venice. He had been staring at the two bags off and on since last Friday. They were trying to tell him something. He could feel it.

The victim had been an old woman who lived alone. The cigarette butt and match were recovered in the kitchen. He and Cassiletti had been called to investigate when the woman's relatives, unable to reach her by phone for two days, had gone to her apartment. That was last Friday. Her car was still in the carport, so the relatives contacted the manager. He used the passkey. They found the woman in the living room, lying lifeless in a puddle of blood, her head dented in. The manager called the police.

Mace and Cassiletti came with their Polaroid camera and notebooks. It was Cassiletti's first homicide investigation. Judging by the degree of rigor mortis, the woman had been dead for at least a full day.

"Murder," Mace explained to his initiate as they perused the crime scene, "is one of the easier crimes to solve. Ninety percent of the assailants are known to the victims. The question is to determine the motive and then work back from there."

They walked through the apartment. St. John pointed out the rifled drawers, the missing wallet from the woman's purse. Her driver's license was sitting out on the otherwise-empty kitchen counter. Mace placed it in an evidence envelope, careful not to touch the surface. They took pictures of the death scene. The woman's family said she didn't smoke. The detectives bagged the cigarette butt and match.

"So how do we determine motive?" He continued his lecture. "We work with what we got. In this case, it's the victim and the scene of the crime. We'll start with her. Female, seventy-two years old, lives alone." He pointed to the dead-bolt locks on her door. "A cautious woman, yet she allowed her attacker inside." He studied her clothing. Her shoes were worn but well cared for. Her dress was handmade, in the style of the thirites. He went through her desk and even went to the parking structure to inspect her car. She was on Social Security, and according to a Medicare form, a widow. Her car was a 1962 Skylark with only twelve thousand miles on it. "What have we got here?"

Cassiletti stuttered a nervous answer. "A little old lady who didn't drive much?"

"Good, good. Now take it a step further."

Cassiletti flipped frantically through his notes.

"She went through the Depression, right?" Mace took over again. "Probably didn't trust banks. Did you see a bankbook?"

"No, sir."

"She probably paid her bills with cash. She collected Social Security; that means she got her check yesterday, like Digger. Where did she cash it? Did she cash it? Where's the money? Her mailbox was empty, which means that yesterday's mail was picked up."

"So the motive was robbery, right?" Cassiletti had an adolescent girl's habit of making every statement into a question.

"Probably. Acting on that assumption, we have more questions. How did the killer know the old lady had money?"

"Maybe he figured like you. That it was the time of the month that she'd be getting her check?"

"Take it a step further."

"He knew her?"

"Now you're talking. Let's start ringing some doorbells."

The investigation hadn't proceeded much further. None of the neighbors had been home. The building was occupied by mostly singles who worked during the day. No one even knew the old lady's name. The detectives found a store in walking distance that cashed checks. If the old lady had cashed her check there on Thursday, it would have been deposited in the store's bank account on Thursday afternoon. By the time the detectives located the bank, it was already after three on Friday, so the bank was closed. The day's deposits would be unavailable till Monday, when the bank opened or the owner of the store returned.

On Friday night, Mace had tracked down the owner through a relative whom he found by going through the phone book, exhibiting the tenacity that had earned him the nickname "the Hound Dog." The relative knew where the man went for the weekend and Mace convinced the relative that it was urgent that he speak to him before the trail got too cold. Mace finally got hold of the store owner at a cabin in Big Bear and learned that the woman had not cashed her check at his store as she usually did. Possibly because the man had closed early to get a jump on the weekend traffic.

There were no prints found on the driver's license, the purse, or the rifled drawers.

His investigation reached the proverbial cul-de-sac.

Now, sitting at his desk, Mace turned the bags over. "What are you trying to tell me?" he asked out loud.

"Talking to yourself? That's a bad sign. Don't tell that shrink."

Mace looked up to see the face of Ernie Potts. Mace covered his eyes with his hand and asked in mock alarm, "God, have you gotten balder? The glare is killing me."

"What you got there?" Ernie asked, ignoring the insult and pointing to the evidence bags.

"Something . . . I don't know what." Mace pulled a matchbook out of his pocket. Holding the pack in his left hand, he lit match after match, blowing them out and letting them drop on the blotter in front of him.

"Good work on Sunday," Ernie said, watching the matches drop to the desktop. "Next time, give me a call. You're making me look bad."

"Wouldn't want to do that."

"It's my case now. I'd hate to write you up for interfering with an investigation."

"Seems like your investigation needed a little interference."

"Don't cross me, buddy."

"You gonna tell your big brother on me?" Mace kept his shoulders loose. Ernie had the advantage of being upright, but his two years with RHD had left its mark. He had put on weight, gotten out of shape.

"My brother has nothing to do with this."

"But him being the commissioner hasn't hurt you, either."

Ernie smiled; he wasn't easily ruffled. "You just be a good boy from now on and pass on any new information relating to the Ballona case."

If Ernie patted him on the head, Mace was going to deck him. Still smiling, Ernie said, "Lighten up, bunkie. I just stopped by to say you did good."

Mace smiled back, letting the moment pass. He shrugged modestly and said, "It was just one of those hunch things, luck really." He turned his attention back to his matches. On the fifth match, Mace spotted what had been nagging at him. He picked up the matchbook again, this time holding it in his right hand and tearing the matches loose with his left. There it was. The bottom of the matches torn using his right hand had flat bottom edges and the tear in the cardboard angled in on the left. The matches torn using his left hand were ripped on the bottom right. The match in his evidence bag, shiny side up, was ripped on the bottom right. He felt a familiar twist of excitement.

"Hound Dog's on the scent again," Ernie said.

"You see it?"

"Sure, the guy's left-handed."

Mace stared at Ernie. "You saw that? Bullshit. You saw me

using my left hand. Listen, I want to take a ride, check something out. I got a new guy I'm breaking in. Want to go with us? We can dazzle the rookie with our combined brilliance."

Ernie adjusted his thick glasses and straightened his bow tie. Mace knew Ernie liked to believe that the bow tie was his trademark. A legend in his own mind. The RHD was going to his head. It wasn't like the guy needed any help in believing in his own greatness.

"Yeah, I'll ride along," Ernie said. "If you needed my help, you should've just asked."

"Cassiletti," Mace yelled to his trainee across the bull pen. "I want you to meet someone."

THEY took an official vehicle, a dark green Polaris with lights in the back window and a diamond-circled *E* in the license plate. Mace drove; Ernie rode shotgun. Cassiletti shifted anxiously in the backseat.

First, they drove over to the Glenwood Garden Apartments. Mace cruised in ever-widening circles until he found a little mom-and-pop operation a few blocks away. It was a small market that sold a smattering of basics: cereal, coffee, cake mixes, canned food, liquor, and cigarettes. Mace parked the vehicle and told Cassiletti to wait for them.

The owner of the market was sitting on a stool behind his counter, judiciously placing himself between the pint bottles and his customers. The racks of cigarettes were in easy reach over his head. His stool swiveled, allowing him access to everything he needed without ever having to leave his cash register or the pistol that Mace knew he kept beneath the counter.

The detective knew the store well. It had been robbed four times in the last year. He entered the store and greeted the owner.

"Morning, Mr. Dunkley. Any trouble lately?"

"Nah, it's been quiet." The man shrugged his shoulders. "It's still early."

"You still cash checks here?"

"If they buy something," Dunkley said. "They gotta have proper ID, of course."

"Of course they do," Ernie agreed in a theatrical voice. Mace shot him a look.

"Dunkley's okay," Mace told Ernie. "He's just trying to make a living." Mace turned back to the store owner. "You remember an old lady who came in here Thursday?"

"We had a lot of old ladies on Thursday."

Mace showed Dunkley a picture of the woman.

Dunkley studied it for a moment. "I can't be sure. Maybe she was in here."

"You sell many Viceroys?" Mace asked.

"Not too many."

"You got any regulars around here who buy them?"

"Four or five."

"You think you can give me any names?"

"My delivery boy for starters—he smokes Viceroys."

"Is he here?"

"Yeah, he's in the back, putting away stock."

"Mind if I have a word with him?"

Dunkley shrugged again. "Go ahead."

The two detectives pushed aside the rubber flaps that separated the market from the storage room. They found the kid unpacking cans of refried beans into a shopping cart. A surfer, he had long blond tangles of sun-bleached hair and deeply chapped lips. The boy reached with his left hand. Ernie nodded to Mace. Mace went back out to the car and told Cassiletti that he had a suspect.

Cassiletti was a dark-haired, light-skinned Italian—a giant of a man: six three and weighing in at 240. He had thick black eyebrows that came together in a widow's peak at the bridge of his nose, making him appear somewhat sinister. When he opened his mouth, the illusion was shattered. People's first reaction was usually to stifle a smile. Tony Cassiletti had a pronounced lisp and an unfortunate high-pitched giggle that bubbled out of him when he was nervous or unsure of himself. In Mace's limited experience with the man, that was most of the time.

"Don't open your mouth," he told him now. "Just follow our lead."

"Sure, Sarge."

"Just drive us to the station and look menacing."

Mace went back into the store. The boy now worked in the narrow aisles, stacking the cans of beans on the shelves. Ernie stood farther down the aisle and studied the recipes on a box of Bisquick.

"Son?"

The kid looked up. Mace flipped out his shield and noted that the veins in the kid's neck bulged suddenly. Ernie smiled and drew a thumb across his throat behind the kid's back.

"Would you come with me?"

"What's this about?" The kid blinked repeatedly as he spoke.

"I have some questions for you. Come on." Mace led the way, the boy trailed, and Ernie fell in behind, sandwiching the kid between them.

The boy raised his hands high in the air in a dramatic gesture, meaning, I've been framed. But it was too early for words; he hadn't been accused of anything. Instead, he shook his head side to side, sighed, and rolled his eyes up in his head. He opened his mouth and muttered something about "Police harassment." They had reached the sidewalk by then. Cassiletti took his cue and delivered a look that silenced the boy. They all piled in the car.

The four drove in silence. The boy stared out the window of the sedan sullenly. Once or twice, he tried to speak, but Mace stopped him with a finger to his lips and pointed at Cassiletti. Ernie did the same. They pulled into the station parking lot and headed for the back entrance. A four-inch-thick steel door guarded the driveway leading to the bowels of the police station. Cassiletti pushed the button of a remote control and the door rose with a shudder. The boy's forehead glistened now with a fine sheen of perspiration. They exited the car. Mace took the boy's arm and led him to an interrogation room. He sat the boy down and left him alone for ten minutes.

"Cassiletti," Mace said, "observe and learn." When he returned, he was holding the bags of evidence from his desk. He gestured to the door like an usher and said to Ernie, "Mistro?"

"Hey, let's give him a lie-detector test," Ernie said. Cassiletti's face had a baffled look, something that was quickly becoming *his* trademark.

Mace shook his head. "God, I haven't pulled that one since . . ." But Ernie was already gone, collecting copying paper and writing "TRUE" and "FALSE" on alternate sheets in big block letters.

"I'm ready," he said finally, and the three men entered the interrogation room. Cassiletti stood by the door, wearing his best "I'm gonna eat you for lunch, punk" expression and remaining obediently silent.

"Kid, I'm going to level with you." Mace put a foot up on the seat of the wooden chair between the kid's legs and leaned into his face. "I think you beat and robbed the old lady. I think she let you in because you had a delivery for her; maybe she'd left something at the store." He held up the bag holding the filter. "I've called a judge to get a warrant for a saliva sample from you. It should be coming in any second. When we get a match, it's going to put you at the murder scene. Do you want to tell me what happened?"

The boy licked his lips and shot his eyes around the room.

"You got the right to remain silent, but that ain't gonna help you. You know that right? I'm offering you a chance to cooperate. You got the right to remain silent, the right to an attorney. What do you think an attorney is going to say when he sees this evidence? He's gonna tell you to deal. Why should we deal if you don't cooperate? If you cannot afford an attorney, one will be provided for you. What kind of mouthpiece do you think you're gonna get for free? Do you understand all these rights?"

The kid nodded.

Mace handed the kid a Miranda form. "Sign here."

Ernie loaded his papers facedown into the feed tray of the copy machine in the corner. "Bring him over here," he ordered.

Mace graced the sweating kid with a sympathetic look.

"Put your hand on the lie detector," Ernie said, pointing at the Xerox machine.

The kid did as instructed.

"Just answer yes or no," Ernie said. "Do you work at Dunkley's Liquor?"

"Yes."

Ernie hit the copy button and the machine spit out a paper that read "TRUE."

"Have you ever committed a felony?" Ernie asked.

"No."

This time, the machine spewed forth a sheet that read "FALSE."

Ernie held up the accusing page. "Let's try that one again."

The next time, the kid said, "Yes" in reply to the same question, and the machine obliged with a page that read "TRUE."

The kid dissolved into tears. "I didn't go there to kill her. She had all that money and wasn't going to give me a tip. I used my own car to bring her back her ID. She should have given me something."

Mace turned to Cassiletti and flashed a victory grin. The boy went on to explain in vivid detail what had happened. It always amazed Mace how these guys would talk, burying themselves. Thank God the bad guys were so dumb. He turned on the tape recorder and had the kid repeat his statement for the record.

Cassiletti caught up to Mace in the hallway after they had turned the kid over to be processed.

"How did you get a judge to act on the evidence so quickly?"

"I didn't."

"Is that fair, what you did?"

"Where did you get this kid?" Ernie asked. Cassiletti started to say something in response, then obviously thought better of starting a verbal duel where he was so plainly outgunned. Ernie raised an amused eyebrow.

Mace took pity and explained. "It's called reasonable deception, kid."

"You gotta know when to hold 'em," Ernie said. Mace groaned, anticipating the next line. Ernie didn't disappoint him. "And know when to fold 'em." Ernie shook his head and laughed. "Fair, he wants to be fair."

AFTER Ernie left to go back to whatever important thing he did at the RHD, Mace pulled out his Ballona file. The girl still needed a name. The deputy coroner had yet to come up with anything. Every set of fingerprints from missing girls reported in January had been checked against the impressions they had. They were now able to restrict their search to Caucasian females five three to five six, 114 to 130 pounds, between the ages of fourteen and twenty-five. The question still remained of whether he was dealing with two victims or three. Because the body fluids of the second arm and now the legs had been so contaminated by salt water, Carol assured him that enzyme tests and PGM subtyping were impossible. Body hairs were also inconclusive.

Mace scanned the list of missing persons. Of the many young women absent without leave, most were never reported; many were runaways, lost somewhere in a psychedelic haze. The families would hold off getting the police involved, hoping their child would return on her own. He noted a new name on the list: Victoria Glassen. There were no fingerprints supplied, just a photograph of a young girl in a high school graduation gown. She fit the physical parameters: female, Caucasian, nineteen years old, five four, 120 pounds. She was a sophomore at Loyola and had been last seen when she left her parent's home in Westchester to go partying with unknown persons on January twenty-ninth.

"Cassiletti, I've got a personal errand to do. I'll be back in about an hour."

"Sure, Sarge." Cassiletti hovered over Mace's desk. "Ernie said they used to call you 'Hound Dog.' What did you call him?"

"Putz." Mace stood up and pulled on his sports coat. "You want a nickname, too?"

"No?"

Mace shook his head and grabbed the piece of paper with the Glassens' address on it. The Glassens' home was on a quiet street. Mrs. Glassen met him at the front door. The strain of the last few weeks showed on her face. He didn't tell her that he was with Homicide—no point in worrying her needlessly. She took him to Vicky's room and watched while he picked up her hairbrush by the bristles and dropped it in a paper bag. She didn't ask why when he asked for a pair of the girl's shoes. If the fingerprints matched, he didn't want to have to return to the house and tell the parents that he had an arm of their missing child but was still working on the rest.

An hour later, he had his answer. Not only did her fingerprints match but the balls and heels of the plaster of Paris feet cast from the legs recovered on Sunday fit perfectly into indentations worn into the inner soles on a pair of her loafers. That confirmed it. Three of the body parts belonged to one person: Victoria Glassen. The file had a name.

The parents supplied him with a list of Vicky's friends. The friends confirmed that the young woman liked to take a walk on the wild side and had a tendency to go off on binges. This explained why the family had waited a week before filling out a missing person's report.

Now he had a name, a face, and, after meeting the grieving parents, a sense of loss. But the case had become personal long before he knew her identity. The fact that the victim was a young girl was always tragic; that tragedy was compounded by the brutal way in which she had been killed. Every policeman going through the Academy at one time studies the case file on the infamous Black Dahlia murder, the homicide of aspiring actress Elizabeth Short. Her corpse was found nude, severed in half, with all the blood drained and the organs removed. Like all unsolved murders, the case was still open—even thirty years later.

The press could be counted on to dramatize the situation further. They would raise the girl's status to something akin to sainthood. He could see the headlines now: BEAUTIFUL YOUNG GIRL BRUTALLY BUTCHERED; MURDER MOST FOUL. They would print her picture and as many gory details as they could pump out of the press relations people. The detective who brought the criminal to justice would have his career made. Mace just wanted the scumbag caught. He wanted out of a city that could produce such a monster. He wanted the guy, and he wanted him to resist arrest.

As requested, he passed this new information on to Parker Center.

AT 11:45, Mace returned to his desk. A statue of a pig wearing a uniform with his badge number on it held down the latest paperwork that needed his attention. He blocked out the confusion of sound around him. Phones rang nonstop; somewhere a prisoner wailed. He was accustomed to the mayhem of the bull pen. Fluorescent lights blazed twenty-four hours a day amid the flirting, banter, and occasional flare of temper. His status of sergeant didn't rate him a private office. Not even the lieutenant was given more than a desk slid against a wall rather than up against another desk.

He shuffled through the staggering amount of paperwork of ten ongoing investigations. The paper that interested him the most was the typed single-spaced report just in. It was written by Dr. Hymie Miller, an independent psychiatrist the station had hired. Copies would need to be forwarded to Parker Center when Mace got around to it.

Consulting with Dr. Miller had been Mace's idea. He knew

that police departments had been putting together psychiatric profiles for some time, though it wasn't an entirely accepted practice. Not sure where to begin, he had called his ex-wife. She was surprised that he even knew she was dating a shrink. He reminded her that he was a detective, after all. When he thought again about turning the report over to Parker Center, he decided not to bother. They probably wouldn't be interested. They had their own experts.

The doctor had put together an impressive amount of information on the Ballona Creek Butcher. Dr. Miller's speculations were limited by the lack of torso, he wrote in a cover note, specifically the information of possible sexual assault and actual cause of death. With the information provided, certain conclusions could be arrived at. The killer hated his victim, but whether this hate was directed at all women or the victim in particular, he really couldn't say. The murderer's lack of regard for human suffering suggested an antisocial psychopathy of an extreme degree. The first arm showed evidence that it had been severed while life remained in the body. Sadistic. The report suggested they look for a man with a strong drive to inflict pain upon women, or to obtain some sort of revenge. The small-caliber bullet fired into a nonlethal part of the body might reflect the man's need to penetrate his victim in a painful manner. Because of the physical effort needed to commit the crime, and assuming the offender worked alone, they should look for a well-proportioned individual, probably between the ages of thirty-five and forty-five. Even without a death scene to examine, it was clear a great deal of preparation had gone into the commission of these acts. Gathering the paraphernalia necessary to sever the arms and legs would have taken planning and foresight. This was not an act that evolved casually. The murderer was also a man of some caution, evidenced by the pains he took to conceal his crime. He would feel no remorse for his crime. The doctor recommended looking for a man whose twisted ideation went back to childhood. Per-

76

haps a search for prior similar atrocities? Attached to the doctor's report was a paper he had published on psychopaths.

Psychopaths, the doctor wrote, were almost two-dimensional, lacking depth of emotion. They went through life miming feelings when other people's reactions clued them to the appropriate expressions. It was as if they had learned the steps to a dance but could never feel the beat. They were pathological liars. The only right and wrong they seemed to distinguish was that when they got caught, it was wrong. Freed, as it were, from the normal restraints of remorse, shame, empathy, love—the feelings that kept the remainder of society within some sort of bounds—the psychopath was capable of monstrous deeds.

That certainly fit the profile, Mace agreed.

Forensics had determined that the force that yanked the limbs from the torso had come simultaneously from opposing directions. Mace looked at his stack of matches, thought of the jagged edges of the body parts, the torn skin and muscles. The condition of the blood in the capillaries of the legs proved that Vicky's heart had ceased to beat just prior to separation. She must have already suffered a great deal, so that was a small consolation. They weren't sure about the second arm.

At twelve o'clock, the ballistics report from the Mancini homicide arrived by messenger. Mace stared at the results and realized with a sickening certainty that the screwup at the bar wasn't going to be forgotten or forgiven for a long, long time. Certainly not by him.

The distinctive scoring scrolled on the bullets retrieved from the head of Flower George matched the rifling marks on the bullet recovered in the leg muscle of the Ballona Creek victim. He had let their first strong lead slip out a bathroom window.

"Cassiletti," he barked, "get over here."

"What's up, boss?"

"We need to go over to the house of the victim we pulled in from Venice the other day. Mancini, George. Run everything we

77

got on that glass and the coat we got from the bar: saliva, hair fibers. I want that van taken apart, too."

"What are we looking for?"

"Vicky Glassen's fingerprints. Tell them to check blood and hair fibers. We're going to turn the place upside down. I want the weapon. I want the hooker. Drop everything else." He stopped; there was that nagging feeling again. "Call the lab and ask them to run the Mancini blood for traces of venereal disease. Never mind—I'll call Carol myself. I want her to check the ends of the Glassen bones for hack marks. She might have overlooked that. I wonder if she can test the body parts for VD?"

"Uh, sir?" Cassiletti waited nervously for Mace to look up. "That isn't our case anymore?"

8

On Tuesday morning, Munch emerged from the bushes half an hour before she was due to be at work. She passed by the Denny's and looked up to see Ruby's cheerful face. The waitress beckoned to her.

What is this broad's problem? Munch thought.

Munch pushed through the glass doors and took a seat at the counter near the door, with her back to the side of the restaurant. Without being asked, Ruby set a mug in front of her and filled it with coffee. "Cream?"

"Black."

"Have you ever tried it with cream and sugar? It's a little more satisfying that way. Look, tell you what. Try a cup like that, and if you don't like it, I won't charge you."

Ruby poured the cream in the coffee till it took on a caramel hue and then poured in two packets of sugar. Munch took a sip. It *was* better.

"I saw you at the meeting yesterday." Ruby patted her hand. "I just want you to know that you're not alone."

She pulled back her hand. "Listen, I'm not that way. I want to be alone."

"That's cool, I was the same way."

"What happened?"

79

"I got some time under my belt. I learned to trust."

Trust. This broad probably believed in the tooth fairy, too. Ruby went to the booths to take some trucker's order. Munch gulped down her coffee. She wanted to leave before Ruby got back and things got any more personal. The coffee was hot and burned all the way down. There was a basket of cellophane-wrapped crackers on the counter, so she helped herself and left a buck for the coffee.

When Happy Jack got to work, she was sitting on the front steps waiting for him.

"I got my Social Security number," she said. "They wanted me to take a test before I could get my driver's license."

"Good morning."

She paused, unsure of herself. Had she been rude? "Good morning."

"So what's the holdup?"

"It's been so long that I have to take the test again in my own car, and it's down."

"What's wrong with it?"

"Timing chain. It's a Pontiac with ninety thousand miles on it; you know how those nylon sprockets like to strip."

"Well, let's tow it in here and get it going. Is it far?"

"Just a few blocks. I figured I'd do it after next Friday."

Happy Jack put his palm over his mouth as she had seen him do that first day. After a minute, his eyes brightened. "Listen, the parts won't cost but about twenty bucks. I'll call Danny over at Fox Tow. He won't charge me anything. Hell, I give him enough business. I'll let you have the parts on credit. You can work on your car when you're between jobs. Sound fair?"

She nodded.

If Happy Jack had been paying close attention, he would have recognized *the look*. It was very similar to the adoring gaze Missy, their dog, often fixed on his wife.

Later that morning, Happy Jack came into the lube room, where she was working on a Pinto with leaking wheel cylinders.

He watched her work for a minute before he said anything. She was aware of him standing behind her and it made her nervous. Was he waiting for her to screw up? She was getting ready to spin around and challenge him when he spoke.

"So what do you do for fun?" he asked.

"Fun? What do you mean?"

"What do you like to do for entertainment? When you're not working?"

She would have preferred he ask her something easy—like the theory of relativity and what it meant to her—at least something she had an answer for. The back of her neck began to burn. He would find her out. She didn't belong here. It had been a mistake to hire her. It was only a matter of time. He didn't know her and when he did . . . Entertainment? It was almost funny. Entertainment was her middle name. If she never did anything but work for the rest of her life, she'd still probably never get even. She straightened her back and glared at him. Fuck it, she thought. If he wanted her to go, he would have to say so. "I don't know," she finally answered through clenched teeth.

"Yeah, I know what you mean," he said. "I spend so much time at work that when I get home, all I want to do is sleep and watch TV."

He left to go back in the office and she stared after him. How much longer would she be able to keep up this charade? If her failure was inevitable, why wait?

At ten o'clock, Cowboy from Fox Tow pulled into the lot.

"Understand you got a comp for me," he said to Jack as he swung down from his truck with an easy grace. He was angularly built, clean-shaven, in his early twenties.

"My mechanic here thinks she threw a timing chain." With a twinkle in his eye, he added, "*She'll* show you where it is."

"She?"

"Daisy, this here is Cowboy. He'll take good care of you."

She looked at him suspiciously. "This won't cost nothing, right?"

"Friendly little thing, ain't she?" Cowboy laughed and turned to her. "I'll only charge a smile, darling."

"Forget it," she said, and started to walk away.

"I was kidding. Shit, you'd think I was trying to get in your pants or something. Don't you worry. I like my women with a little meat on their bones. I also prefer it if they don't smell like ninety weight."

She glared at him, suddenly embarrassed. For an awful second, she felt like she might cry again or something. What was happening to her?

"All right," Jack intervened. "Let's kill the chitchat. I got a business to run. Daisy, get your keys and let's get this over with."

"I left the keys in the car. It wasn't going nowhere."

"Come on, girl," Cowboy waved, seated back in the driver's seat. "Let's go get you hooked up."

She climbed in to the cab with him and directed him to where her car was hidden.

When they got there, he let out a low whistle. "Dang, girl, you sure know how to make things rough on an old country boy."

"You're from the country?"

"You don't think I made this hillbilly accent up, do you? Where are you from, Mars?"

Despite herself, she smiled. "Close."

"There, that's more like it. Was that so hard?"

She turned to face the car again. "Maybe we can push it out into the street."

Cowboy looked at her critically. "It's a pretty heavy car for just two of us to push uphill. Don't worry, I'll manage. I've been doing this awhile. You're lucky this was so well hidden. If a cop had spotted it in this neighborhood, I would have had to impound it."

She froze. "You work for the cops?"

"Why? You wanted or something?"

"No," she said quickly, then added lamely, "I just thought they had their own tow trucks."

"They sub out the towing. It's a good contract; we get paid for the tow and we get all our tickets fixed." He smiled at her. "You ever get any tickets you need fixing, you just come see me."

"First, I need a license," she said, and thought, And what I need fixing goes beyond what a traffic cop can do for me.

They drove back to the shop in silence. Jack told her that she might as well get started on her car while business was slow. At noon, he tapped her on the shoulder and told her to take a break.

"Come and sit; have some lunch. We still need to decide what flowers to plant here. It gets pretty hot in the summer. We need something that can take the heat."

She washed up and went to join the two men.

"That Cowboy is a real nice fellow," Jack said, opening his brown lunch sack.

"I suppose." She pulled a package of broken bread sticks from her pocket.

"What's the matter, Daisy?" Lou asked. "Isn't he your type? Maybe you should meet his boss, Lee. Yeah, maybe I'll introduce the two of you."

"Will you look at this?" Jack said, holding up two sandwiches. "Is my wife trying to get me fat, or what? I can't eat all this. Help me out, Daisy."

She snatched the sandwich greedily. It was roast beef on white, with lettuce and lots of mayonnaise. She ate three bites quickly before she spoke again. "This Lee ain't a cop, is he?"

Lou laughed. "No, and Lee ain't a he, either."

Between bites, she snarled, "Go fuck yourself."

"How about the mouth on her?" Lou said.

Jack intervened. "All right, that's enough of that. Do I have to baby-sit you two? Listen, Daisy, Cowboy gave me a couple of tickets for the rodeo this weekend. You want to go? Maybe bring a friend?"

She very carefully showed no emotion in her face. "You mean a rodeo, like with horses?"

"Yeah, they got horses and bull riding, stuff like that. Interested?"

Horses. She'd love to see horses; maybe they'd let her feed them carrots. "Yeah, I'd like to go. But I'll just need one ticket. It's kind of short notice to call a friend; they're probably all busy."

Jack didn't say anything; he just reached into his shirt pocket and fished out a shiny stub.

9

On Wednesday afternoon, Mace St. John got a call from Carol Zapata at the crime lab. He was staring at the phone and was not surprised when it rang. He answered on the first ring.

"I have some results for you," she said.

"What did you find out?"

"First the bad news. We couldn't run the blood of the Glassen girl; it's been too long. Also, there wasn't enough saliva left on the glass to tell anything about your suspect. I even checked the sweat on the collar of the coat, but I'm afraid your perp isn't a secreter. So, no luck. I did find some hack marks on the bones. I figured they were shovel marks. By the way, the Mancini corpse tested positive for gonorrhea. Anything else that you want me to check for? The body is going to be cremated later today."

"Nothing I can think of."

Her tone changed, became softer. "How's Digger?"

"He has his good days. Thanks for asking." He told her he'd check with her later, then hung up.

Mace flipped open his notebook and turned back pages till he came to the section devoted to the Glassen murder. He went over what he had all ready. Victim was young, pretty, and, according to her friends, a party girl. He made a note to question her friends about her health, specifically venereal disease. "Boyfriends?" his notes asked. He'd come up with the name of only one boy at the college. It seemed that she did the majority of her socializing off campus. According to her friends, she liked a rough crowd. So what did he have? The solution of the mystery hinged on asking the right questions. There were many. For starters, why the bullet? Maybe the perp needed to silence the girl. Maybe he'd decided to put her out of her misery sooner. Why the mutilation? Was there a sexual assault? He underlined "Torture," and wrote next to it, "Satanic ritual (?)." If an investigation took a wrong turn early, a detective could waste a lot of time on a path that led nowhere. Early assumptions could be damaging, even disastrous.

He flipped forward to his current investigation. On the page devoted to the Mancini murder, he made a note of the venereal disease. The question of motive on that one was almost immaterial. When a scumbag like Flower George gets shot, you can almost write it off to inevitable. He read the guy's sheet again. Contributing, statutory rape, pandering—a real sweetheart. Cassiletti had a point: The girl deserved a commendation. But it wasn't a perfect world, and, as he tried to explain to Caroline Rhinehart, murder was murder.

He dropped the well-worn binder on his desk and a Polaroid fluttered to the floor. Cassiletti, on his way over to have St. John sign a report, picked it up. Before returning the photograph, he glanced at it. In his resulting shock, he almost dropped it, as if discovering it were coated with some contagious deadly virus.

"God, what is this?"

Mace chuckled and took the picture back.

"Didn't I ever tell you the story of Smiley here?"

"No."

"Five years ago, patrolmen called in a suspicious death. Smiley hadn't showed up for work in three days and her boss went over to her place to look for her. Her car was still in the garage and her door was locked—one of those dead-bolt types that lock from the inside. The boss called the cops, and the patrolmen felt they had probable cause to kick in the door.

"They found Smiley here in the bathroom, obviously deceased. The watch commander called me. I got there and took pictures, made notes. Her bed was freshly made and there were recently washed sheets in the bathtub. Smiley was on the bathroom floor and there was blood everywhere. Next to the body were an eight-inch butcher knife and a claw hammer. On the laundry hamper were a towel and a straight razor. The razor had also been washed and left on the towel to dry.

"I was there for fifteen minutes when I heard her gurgle. Smiley wasn't dead after all. Smiley was still very much alive. We called the paramedics and they came and took her to the hospital. You can see the airway tube." Cassiletti grimaced at the picture and studied it closer. "The next day, I took her statement." Mace paused for effect. "Written, of course."

Cassiletti only nodded. He wiped his palms on his pants.

Mace continued. "Seems she wanted to kill herself. That much, I had figured. First, she tried to slash her wrists with the razor. She really meant to do it. A lot of times you can see hesitation in the cut marks. Most suicides don't really want to do it. A call for help and all that. This lady was determined. She just cut across instead of down the center." He stopped and pointed to where the arteries ran in his own arm. "She also lifted each breast and made deep half-moon cuts; then she lay on her bed and waited to die. When it didn't happen, she got up and washed the sheets and the razor. Then she went in the kitchen and got the knife and the hammer and did the damage you see here."

Cassiletti stole another look at the photograph. "She lived?"

"You bet. Unluckiest lady I've ever met. She took that knife and drove it into her throat with the hammer, then ripped it across. Missed both jugular veins by a quarter inch, and then she lay there on the floor for three days."

"Why is it all white?" Cassiletti asked. He still couldn't believe that a throat could gape open that far and a person live through it.

"Staph infection," Mace answered.

"Why do you carry this around?"

"I show it to young girls I catch hitchhiking."

Cassiletti shook his head. "Do you know if she tried it again?"

"As a matter of fact, I talked to her about a month ago. She's doing good. She said God wasn't finished with her yet." Mace reached behind his chair for his coat. "Let's take a ride over to the bar. I want to talk to that bartender again."

When they arrived at the Venture Inn, Benny wasn't happy to see them. "Man," he told Mace, "your people have torn my place apart. I warned you to stay away from that little broad. She's nothing but trouble. I hope you find her before any of the Pride."

"Why are they looking for her?"

"She gave a few of the boys the clap. They don't appreciate that."

"How many?"

"At least six of them."

"She was having relations with six different bikers?"

"I don't know if I'd call it relations, exactly."

Mace looked up and down the deserted bar. "Did we scare away all your customers? Where are all the bikers tonight?"

"Tonight is meeting night, so we won't see them till later."

"Where are all the women?"

"Meeting night ain't a good night for the women to be out." Benny winked. "The boys get a little stirred up, if you know what I'm saying."

"Was it a meeting night when Munch gave all the boys the clap?"

"No, it was this last weekend. The boys were just having some fun. I know most of them. In fact, I served with their president, Crazy Mike, at Chu Lai."

Mace pulled a photograph from his notebook. It was a more recent picture of Victoria Glassen, one that hadn't been released to the press. Her hair was lighter and she was heavily made up, making her appear older and far less innocent. If Potts had gotten hold of one of these, it would soon be plastered all over the place. That was an old trick of his when an investigation was going badly—discredit the victim.

Mace took a gamble that the patrons of the Venture Inn didn't keep up on local news and wouldn't recognize the girl as a victim. He handed the picture to Benny, who studied it quickly and then declared, "She had ID. I'd swear on a Bible this broad was twenty-one."

Mace's pulse quickened, but his voice remained even, almost slowing to a drawl. "When was she in here?"

"A few weeks ago."

He scratched the back of his ear. "Any reason you remember her so vividly?"

"Yeah, she made it to the trophy wall." Benny pointed to the back wall. Next to the dartboard was a large cork bulletin board filled with memorabilia: female underwear, personalized license plates, and courtesy cards from other bike clubs. Benny limped out from behind the bar and took the detective on a tour. He lifted a pair of torn red nylon panties and showed the detective the photograph underneath.

A very much alive Victoria was dancing. Her arms were above her head and her mouth was open in a lopsided grin. Her blouse was unbuttoned and her tits were on the upswing. Her dance partner had his back to the camera. The red panties were on his head.

"Who's the dude?"

"Shit, I don't remember." Benny laughed. "A prospect. You see, he doesn't have his full colors yet." He shook his shaggy head in admiration and said almost reverently, "She was one game bitch, that one."

Mace studied the picture. It showed a side to Vicky he hadn't seen yet but was quickly imagining. "Mind if I borrow this?"

"Do I have a choice?"

"There're always choices." Mace stretched out his throat, tilting his head back and pointing his chin toward the rough-hewn ceiling. He sighed as if bored, exhaling through his nostrils. When he brought his head back down, it was to stare directly into Benny's eyes. "This girl is nineteen; I really don't think you want the picture of an underage girl on your trophy rack."

"Take it."

Mace pulled the thumbtack out that held the photograph to the corkboard. He pulled an evidence bag from his pocket. Using his pen, he lifted the torn panties and dropped them in the bag. Another picture caught his eye. It was a group shot of the whole club. The biker in the center of the group, the one who had a Prez patch sewed over the pocket of his Levi cutoff, stared back at him. A familiar tattoo peeked out from the sleeve of his T-shirt: *Death Before Dishonor*. One below that read *FTW*, which Mace recognized as standing for "Fuck the world." The biker wore his dark blond hair shorter than most bikers, just to his ears, and, unlike the other club members, he was clean-shaven. "Is this Crazy Mike?"

Benny nodded uncomfortably.

"How long did you serve with him?"

"Only for a month; then I was wounded. Take my advice— you don't want to mess with him."

"I'll keep that in mind," Mace said dryly. "Thanks for your help."

"Don't mention it," Benny said. He gave the detective a sober look. "I mean that."

Cassiletti was waiting for Mace in the car. Mace sat down next to him and flipped open his notebook. He made a notation. "Satan's Pride. Check moniker file."

"Where to now, Sarge?"

"I want to drop this off at the lab. Hopefully, our boy left a calling card." He showed Cassiletti the photograph and panties. "We'll get a blowup of this picture, too. I need an ID on this guy; then we'll put some pressure on him."

"You think the bikers are involved?"

"I think we need to turn over a few rocks and see what crawls out."

10

Wednesday afternoon, Happy Jack called his newest mechanic into the office. "Close the door behind you," he said after Munch cleared the doorway.

She closed the door with the uncomfortable feeling that she was busted. Life had been good for three days in a row. Of course it wouldn't last. I don't care, she told herself—her own personal mantra. If you don't care, who can touch you? The back of her neck burned with sudden anxiety as she realized that that particular piece of wisdom had been taught to her by Flower George.

"Daisy," Jack began, "I know you don't live at the address you gave me. Lou drove by there today and there is no such address."

"Lou was checking up on me?"

"Listen, I just want to help. I can't do that if you're not straight with me. Lou said you were on something. He says that's why you sweat so much and your pupils are so big. I won't have drug use here. I'm gonna ask you once. Do you use drugs?"

She looked him directly in the eye. The secret to good lying is to convince yourself first. "No," she said. If he asked her if she'd ever been arrested, she would answer no with equal sincerity. Daisy Signman had never been arrested. Still, she was glad when he didn't ask her. The question had been on the job application. It had asked if she'd ever been convicted of a crime and she had written, "None," as in "none of their fucking business." But he had asked her about drugs, and she wasn't doing drugs, so it wasn't a lie, and that was all he needed to know. He just wanted to help her, huh? Where had she heard that before? Her probation officer, Ms. Rhinehart, had said the same thing. They all started out that way. But when it came right down to it, you had only yourself. George had taught her that.

She compressed her mouth to a thin line. Why couldn't people just leave her alone? She'd be fine if they'd just stop hassling her. He thought she sweated a lot? So what? It's a free country, right? "Maybe I'm sick" was all she said.

He put a hand on her shoulder and looked into her eyes. "Are you living in your car?"

"Does it matter?" Suddenly, the nagging cramps that had been pestering her for the last few day grew teeth. A searing flash of pain, like an electrical shock, darted across the walls of her abdomen, knocking the breath from her words.

"What's wrong?"

She felt the color drain from her face. "It's just the flu." Her voice sounded funny. "I'll be okay in a couple of days." She started to think maybe she was wrong, that maybe there was something else the matter with her. She'd never had withdrawals that felt like this.

"It's more than the flu." He rushed to her side. "I'm taking you to the hospital."

She wanted to say that she'd be fine, but she was scared now and too busy concentrating on breathing. She nodded her head and allowed him to help her to his car.

At the hospital, she was seen immediately. The first doctor ordered blood and urine tests. The nurse came in to the examining room to draw her blood. Munch offered her right arm; the woman would never find a vein on her left.

"Have you ever had your appendix out?" the doctor asked loudly.

"No." The nurse helped her out of her coveralls and into a

hospital gown. Munch lay on the table, her knees drawn to her chest. The nurse waited in the corner while the doctor slipped on his gloves. He gently pushed her back and began to probe her stomach.

"When was your last period?"

"I don't know, a couple weeks ago, I guess."

"Do you think you're pregnant?"

"I don't think so."

"Do you feel pregnant?"

"How the hell am I supposed to know?" She grimaced. "I feel like someone stuck a beer bottle up me and broke it."

"I'd like to do a pelvic exam," he said. "Scoot down and put your feet in the stirrups."

She did as he asked. She didn't wince as the cold instrument entered her. She had learned long ago to detach from that part of her body. Let them do what they wanted; they were never getting the real her.

"I'm seeing some discharge at the opening to your cervix," he said. "It looks like you have a pretty severe infection here. Is it possible you were exposed to a venereal disease?"

She laughed then, a bitter bark that ended in a coughing fit. "Is that what this is about? I might have clap. I didn't know it could hurt so much."

"If the infection reaches your fallopian tubes and ovaries, it can be very uncomfortable. You should quit smoking," the doctor said. "Those things will kill you."

She laughed again. "When I'm old, right?"

The doctor and nurse left the room. Munch listened to their footsteps retreat down the hall and then she rolled off the table. The first drawers she opened were filled with syringes. Her hand hovered over them. They were clean, still in the packages, and not those orange disposable kind that get so dull after awhile.

Her last outfit had been a disposable insulin syringe. Every time she coaxed one more usage out of the flimsy paraphernalia, she felt like she was playing Russian roulette. The needle had been bent and reshaped so many times, it resembled a corkscrew. The worst was when the hollow metal point bent right at the plastic, at the needle's thickest point. After she straightened it, praying it wouldn't kink, she always worried how many times she had before it broke off. And when it broke, would the needle already be embedded in her vein? She wasn't so much concerned that the broken metal would enter her bloodstream and swim into her heart as she was that the dope would squirt out the broken syringe and be wasted, a dribbling rivulet of bitter brown smack going somewhere where she couldn't lick it up.

She grabbed a handful of syringes and stuck them in the pocket of her coveralls, which were lying on the floor. The drawers in the examining table yielded nothing of interest. Her fingers had just slipped around the stethoscope hanging on the door when she heard footsteps returning. She hopped back up on the table.

"We won't have the results back on your tests for a couple of days," the nurse said when she entered the room. "I'm going to give you some penicillin and we're going to send you home with some pills. It's very important that you take all of them."

"What kind of pills?"

"Antibiotics. Roll over, please." The nurse took the cap off a large syringe and swabbed Munch's hip with an alcohol-soaked cotton ball. "You're going to feel a slight sting."

"I don't mind."

The doctor knocked before entering the room, which she thought was kind of funny, considering. "Assuming this infection is gonorrhea, I'm afraid there's a good chance that you might have some scarring on your fallopian tubes." The doctor had trouble meeting her eye. "You might not be able to have children."

"I don't care." She hopped down from the table. "That's good when you think about it. I mean, who wants kids anyway?" He acted like it were the end of the world or something. She rubbed her butt where they had given her the shots, kneading the two hard knots that had formed there. She didn't want to say any-

94

thing, but they burned like hell. "Can I go now?"

The nurse took her hand. "Before you go, you need to talk to a lady from the Health Department. She's very nice. Her name is Mrs. Canopolis." The nurse paused at the doorway and gave her a long, sad look. "Daisy, take all the medicine. Come back in a week and we'll take another blood test. No sex until then, all right?"

"No problem. Sew it shut if you want. I don't care."

The woman from the Health Department took her to an office. She had Munch look at graphic photographs of people in various stages of infection. There were men with swollen testicles, woman with rashes, and babies born with holes in their palates. Munch studied the pictures with interest.

"We're trying to head off an epidemic," the woman said. "Do you understand the importance of treating this disease?"

"I guess so."

"I need you to write down all the sexual partners you've had contact with in the last month. Addresses and phone numbers would be very helpful, too. Don't worry. We'll be very discreet. If and when we contact these people, we never reveal the source of our information. If you want, you can contact them yourself and they can seek treatment."

"You want last names, right?"

"Yes, dear."

"I don't know any."

"Can you give me physical descriptions?"

"You're asking a lot." She looked at the pictures again. "They'll know soon enough, right?"

"With gonorrhea, men can develop symptoms within a few days: pain with urination, discharge."

"Serves the bastards right, don't you think?"

"I'm not here to make judgments." The woman smiled kindly and then shook her head. "Regardless, even if they seek treatment, it might not be until after they've infected new partners. Woman can go longer without knowing anything is wrong. They can be totally asymptomatic, like you probably were. By the time the disease is detected, the damage to their body can be devastating. Besides, what about the man who infected you? Don't you wish he had gotten himself treatment?"

Munch didn't answer; she just fixed an unfathomable look on the woman, her big orphan eyes wide and glistening. Which man? Which time? Flower George would say that everyone had to look out for themselves, period. All you had to ask yourself was what was in it for you. Made life simple, he said. Yeah, and she wanted to be just like him, right? She reached for the form Mrs. Canopolis offered. "How far back do you want me to go?"

"Two months."

"I'll need more paper."

JACK was waiting for her in the reception area, as nervous as a new father. The nurse held Munch's arm protectively and helped her walk to where he waited. He grabbed her other arm and hovered over her anxiously.

"Remember," the nurse said, handing Jack the bottle of pills, "take them all."

"Don't worry," Jack said. "I'll make sure she does."

They drove back to the station. Munch explained that she had an infection. It was no big deal, she assured him. He watched her walk bent over to her now-operational GTO.

"Are you going to be all right?" he asked.

"I'm feeling better already. I'll be fine. I can handle it." She reassured him with a little smile. She was anxious to get to the DMV before it closed.

"WHAT are you doing here?" Happy Jack asked her the next morning. He frowned and the skin between his eyes folded in on itself.

"I still work here, don't I?" Munch asked guardedly.

96

"How are you feeling? You could barely walk yesterday."

"I'm much better, really." She walked back and forth to prove it. "That medicine they gave me yesterday fixed me right up."

"Are you taking the pills?"

"Yeah, I even doubled up on them. Figured they'd work faster that way."

"I don't think that's a good idea. Just take them like they said."

"Don't worry, 'cause I can handle it," she said. "What I need right now is some work. What have you got for me?"

He went inside the office and grabbed a clipboard. "We got a Dodge Charger with a rough idle. I think the guy dropped a cylinder." He handed her the keys and asked again, "You sure you're up to this?"

"Believe me, I'm good as new." She turned from him as a stab of pain hit her somewhere just over her bladder. She took a breath and the spasm passed. The Dodge was parked under the pine tree. She started it up and pulled the spark-plug wires off one at a time, till she found the dead cylinder.

"You ever use a scope?" Jack asked her, watching from the office.

"Never needed one," she said.

"Lou will show you how to hook it up." Jack lumbered down the stairs. "Lou, come over here. Show her how this contraption works." Then to Munch, he added, "It'll save you from getting shocked."

Lou demonstrated how to hook up the various wires and how to read the monitor. He threw her the owner's manual. "Here, read this. In a week, you'll be telling me how to work it."

She held the manual in her hand and acknowledged his help with a mumbled "Thanks." By tomorrow, she'd know more than he ever had. She'd always been good with books. It used to blow Wizard's mind how she remembered everything she read. He said she should run the numbers, because she'd never have to write anything down. She preferred to fix things.

Using the diagnostic machine, she shorted out a cylinder at a time. Then she traced the one that didn't alter the idle speed when the spark to it was diverted. A compression test on the dead cylinder confirmed her suspicions. She told Jack the head would have to come off, that a valve was burned or stuck open.

"I'll call the customer," he said.

Ten minutes later, Jack emerged from the office. "The guy wants to come over and see for himself. Think you can handle a valve job?" he asked her. "The heads are heavy. I don't want to see you trying to lift them by yourself. You're gonna hurt yourself if you do. Ask me or Lou to help you. That's what we're here for, to help one another. Okay?"

"I never needed help before." She wiped the wrench in her hand clean. "I've always managed."

"Well, we're team players here."

They were interrupted by the phone ringing.

"I'll get it," Lou called. He picked up the extension in the lube room. "Jack, this lady says she's a member of AA and wants to know if we're AA-approved." He laughed and returned to the call.

"She meant to say triple A." Jack smiled. "Happens all the time. Lou just likes to embarrass the people. Listen, I know he's an asshole, but if you get past that, you could learn a lot from him."

"I'll try," she promised.

She heard a car pull in the driveway behind her. Before she could turn around, Jack was greeting the customer.

"Well, here's a familiar face," he called out over her shoulder. "Hey, Ruby. What can we do for you, doll?" He walked over to the waitress's car and leaned into her window.

Ruby held up her hand to shield her eyes from the sun. "Good morning, Jack. My car is jiggling again. Do you think I need another tune-up?"

"Probably just an adjustment. We tuned it a month ago." He

straightened. "Have you met my new mechanic?" He presented Munch proudly.

"As a matter of fact, I have. She's been into the restaurant a few times, but I never caught her name."

"Daisy, I want you to meet Ruby. Take good care of her; she makes the best coffee in the valley."

Munch nodded and the corners of her mouth did a quick upward jerk.

"Her car is idling rough. Hook it up to the scope and see what you can do."

Munch rolled the scope out to the Datsun and hooked it up as she had been shown; then she got a glass of water and set it on the air cleaner.

"Start it up," she told Ruby. Ignoring the scope, she adjusted the carburetor till the water in the glass stopped shaking.

"Wow, my car's never run this smooth."

"You can shut it off now."

Ruby got out of the car and stood near Munch while she disconnected the scope.

"How many days do you have?"

"What do you mean?"

"How much time sober?"

"I don't drink," Munch moved away from her before she tried anything.

"I'm in AA, too," Ruby said.

"You mean AAA."

"No, AA. That's why I was at the meeting . . . at the church."

"Oh, uh, well, congratulations, I guess."

"Isn't that why you were there?"

"No, I was there to see the priest. I ain't no alcoholic, no offense."

Ruby patted her arm. "I'm not trying to push anything on you. But if you're trying to get clean, you're going to need some help. There's another meeting tonight at the high school. Would you like to go with me?"

"I got plans tonight."

Ruby opened the trunk of her car and fished through a cardboard box. "Here're some meeting directories with the times and addresses of the meetings held near here. The thinner directory is for Narcotics Anonymous meetings; there's a younger crowd that goes there. You know, in case your plans change." She pushed another card in Munch's hand. "You might want to read this."

After she drove off, Jack walked over with a middle-aged man wearing white bell-bottoms and Elvis Presley sideburns. His polyester shirt was open in front, revealing graying chest hairs and a thick gold chain.

Munch studied the man for two seconds before deciding, Fifty, plus.

They came to a stop at the fender of the Dodge. Jack looked up from his clipboard. "Daisy, this is the owner of the Charger. Show him what you found." He went back to work on the estimate.

The customer leered at her. "Daisy, are you the *head* mechanic?" He laughed and elbowed Jack. "Be sure to get all my nuts tight, honey."

Jack pressed his lips together. "Does this look right to you?" he asked, handing her the work order. He pointed to the estimate price. She noticed where he had changed a one to a seven.

"That should cover it," she agreed. She liked his way better.

Jack had the man sign the estimate, and after the guy left, Jack turned to Munch. "What a pig."

"Yeah," she said. "I hate pigs."

11

Thursday afternoon, Mace called Caroline Rhinehart. His heart quickened at the sound of her voice and it took him a second or two to remember why he had called. "The investigation involving the Mancini girl has heated up."

"What's happened?"

"It's been linked to another homicide. I need everything you've got: friends, family, haunts."

"Let me grab her file."

Mace pictured slender fingers opening the file cabinet. He wondered if she played the piano. He had a nineteenth-century practice piano aboard the Bella Donna. It had taken many trips to the music store to get it tuned. The wooden harp that held the strings had been almost hopelessly warped from years of bouncing around on the back of a horse-drawn wagon. That's how they gave lessons in those days—they took the little piano with them from farm to ranch.

Caroline returned to the phone. "Is she a suspect in the other homicide?"

"Certain physical evidence links her to the crime."

"When did this other homicide take place?"

"End of January."

"Oh." There was a pause as he heard her shuffle papers. "I was assigned to her in December. I had her on surprise testing. Except for alcohol, she tested clean, mostly."

"Mostly?"

"I'll get back to that. I helped her get a job at the Venice Cab Company. Her employer was a man named Orson Ozwald; everyone calls him 'Wizard.'

"She was doing well, reporting to our appointments, showing up for work. I really had hopes for her; there was always a certain innocence to her, despite the fact that she grew up on the streets."

"What about other family?" Mace asked.

"The only family I show was the father, now deceased, according to you."

"The cab company is on Brooks and Electric, right?"

"Do you want the number?"

"Nah, that won't be necessary." He paused for a while over the telephone, trying to think of something more to say. Caroline filled in the silence.

"I tested her again last week. As I said, she'd been testing clean. Well, the first test anyway. The second was last week." She hesitated a second, then admitted, "It was dirty. Heroin."

"Were you going to violate her?"

"Probably not. Scare her, maybe. I like to give everyone a chance."

He chewed on her answer for a minute. Did she really mean everyone? "Thanks."

"You're welcome." He listened till he heard her hang up. Then he turned to his waiting partner. "Let's get out of here."

"Where are we going?"

"We're off to see the Wizard."

PLUMES of sparks splashed into the air at the far corner of the open yard of the Venice Cab Company as they pulled in the driveway. A large man bent over the empty gas tank of a Plymouth, at work with his torch. His dark blue jacket with the Ford cobra emblem on one sleeve and the American flag on the other was pocked with burn holes. The top half of his wide ebony face was concealed by a tinted welder's visor. He lifted it when the detectives approached.

Mace imagined that in another time, the big black man would have been the village blacksmith, pounding out horseshoes, keeping his iron hot in vats of billow-stoked coals.

The detectives presented their gold shields. Wizard waved the badges away. "I know who you is." He said this unsmiling, but met their eyes without flinching.

"We're investigating the murder of George Mancini. You probably knew him as Flower George."

"I didn't know that asshole as anything." He turned off the valve on his propane tank and the flame abruptly died. He set down his torch and reached for a piece of steel from a pile on the ground. Turning his back to the detectives, he proceeded with his work.

The detectives followed him to a workbench and watched him spin the handle of a large vise till its jaws opened wide enough to accommodate the iron bar in his hand. "We're seeking an employee of yours, Munch Mancini," Cassiletti said. "When did you see her last?"

The big man faced them. A muscle under his left eye twitched once, almost imperceptibly, before he answered. "I haven't seen her all week. Is she okay?"

Mace twisted his head from side to side, stretching his neck. As he did so, he made a visual sweep of the shop. Against a rear wall sat a bare motorcycle frame. A stout iron ring had been recently welded to the rear strut support; beads of bright silver ringed the junction points, awaiting a coat of primer, then a second of lacquer.

"Did she ever ride with any of the Satan's Pride?" he asked.

"I know she liked bikes. I don't know the people she hung with outside the shop. They come in here. I do some work on their choppers, modifications, you know."

"Stuff like this?" Mace pointed to the frame in the corner.

Wizard stared back. "I don't think the man would appreciate me discussing his business like that." He grabbed the top of the steel bar he had secured in the vise and pulled down on it. The bench shuddered and the piece of steel bowed in the center.

Mace tried a different tack. "Do you know if Munch was on good terms with her father? Had the two ever argued?"

"Why do you do me like that?" the big man said. "First, you tell me the man's dead; then you want to know if the girl was mad at him. I'll tell you one thing—Flower George wasn't about nothing but hisself. I think he was messing with that girl. She never gave him up, wasn't her way." He removed the steel from the vise and used it to punctuate his words as he spoke. "That girl had a future in the automobile business. She picked it up quick, like none of your business." He set down the piece of iron he had been gesturing with on an old couch that sat against the wall. The water-stained cushions depressed with the weight of it. Mace figured that piece of steel had to weigh a good forty pounds, and the man had been waving it around like a majorette's baton. Wizard moved in close to the detectives. Cassiletti took an involuntary step backward. "Why don't you just let it go?" Wizard asked. "Give the girl a break. You can do that."

Mace dropped his chin to his chest and bent slightly at the knees. He took a measure of the big man, looking up at him from a boxer's stance till the whites of his eyes showed beneath his irises. "Give her a message." He held up a hand when Wizard began his protests. "Tell her I just want to know where she got the gun; then all else will be forgotten. Tell her I talked to Ms. Rhinehart and I'll square everything." Mace patted the big man on the chest and felt solid muscle.

"Let's get out of here," he told Cassiletti, and they walked slowly to the car.

When they were in the car, Cassiletti asked, "Would you do that? Forget the whole case?"

"What have we got?" Mace replied. "A corpse, no weapon, no

witnesses, no confession. Of course her prints would be all over the van and the house. She lived there. The best we could hope for is a conviction for joy riding; even that probably wouldn't stick."

"So you'll let her slide?"

"If we play our cards right, she'll help us build our own case. Remember: reasonable deception. Criminals dumb enough to provide evidence and testimony against themselves deserve what they get."

THE Narcotics Anonymous meeting started at 8:30 at a high school in Reseda. Munch slunk in ten minutes late. A large banner that read WE CARE was tacked over the chalkboard. She stood by the back door, ready to bolt.

She liked the sound of Narcotics Anonymous. It sounded tough and hip. She rolled the words around in her head. The people at the meeting didn't look like any addicts she ever knew. They were too happy, almost glowing. They had to be smoking something.

A woman stood at a podium at the front of the room and cleared her throat, then read some stuff from a plastic-bound folder—something called "Who Is an Addict?" Munch didn't need any help with that question. Who an alcoholic was was another issue entirely. The yellow card that Ruby had pushed on her was some kind of test for seeing if you were an alcoholic. The instructions said to answer yes or no. It was a rigged test. Had she ever been arrested for drunk driving? Yes, but she had been off dope that week, so technically, she was doing good. Did she ever drink in the morning? Only beer, but that still counted as a yes. Did she ever hide her liquor? Only if she didn't want some asshole ripping her off. Then a bunch of stuff about if drinking ever interfered with work, social, or family relations. She'd left that answer blank. When she got through with the test, it said on the bottom that you only had to answer yes to a few to be an alcoholic.

The woman at the podium announced that there would be refreshments at the break.

Munch lit a cigarette and looked around the room for an empty seat.

The woman finished reading and the group responded with scattered applause. "Now, it says here I'm supposed to introduce the first speaker." She laughed self-consciously. "Gilbert S. will speak for fifteen minutes about what it was like, what happened, and what it's like now."

A Chicano man with tattoos showing everywhere that his starched and ironed white T-shirt didn't cover rose from his seat in the first row. The people clapped and whistled when he took his place behind the podium. Munch sat in his vacated chair.

He began by telling a story about the time he was low-riding with his homeboys. "We were dropping red and drinking Mad Dog." A chorus of appreciative titters rippled through the audience. "The car flipped on the freeway. We were going sixty miles an hour and I was thrown clear. At the hospital, the doctors told me that I hadn't suffered any serious injury because I was so drunk. My body was so loose when I hit the road that I just absorbed the impact. If I had been tense, they said, I would have had broken bones.

"So, I told my homeys, 'Listen, man, if you're gonna drive, drink; it'll save your life.' " Gilbert waited for the laughter to subside before he continued. He went on to talk about his life of robbing, using, and going to prison. He had been to every penitentiary in California and had spent twelve of his twenty-eight years behind bars. Then, he said, he had found Narcotics Anonymous.

"I'll always be an addict," he said. "Even today, when I get a headache, I tell my wife to give me four aspirin, cuz two ain't gonna get it."

"Why does everyone keep laughing?" Munch asked the man next to her.

"They identify."

She looked around the room.

"Feels good, doesn't it?" he asked.

She was surprised to find herself nodding in agreement. The meeting continued.

She listened openmouthed, as if trying to absorb the speaker's words through every orifice in her head.

Gilbert kept his message simple. "Go to meetings or die," he said. "Go to meetings, meetings, meetings, and don't use in between."

At the end of his talk, everyone clapped. The woman who had read the preamble stood up and said, "We will now observe the seventh tradition." A basket was passed.

Munch watched everyone reach in their pockets and pull out dollar bills. She knew it—they wanted money. What a scam.

"Newcomers and visitors for the first time are asked not to contribute," the woman finished.

At the coffee break, everyone poured into the parking lot. She grabbed a handful of cookies and stood where she could overhear snatches of their conversations:

"How much time you got?"

"Thirty days."

"Great."

"You got a sponsor yet?"

"Henry D. went back out."

"I'm not surprised; the dude wasn't willing to get honest."

"Are you new?" someone asked her.

"I guess so."

"How much time do you have?"

"Four days."

"That's great. Keep coming back," the man said. "Take it a day at a time. Remember, there are no big deals."

The meeting started up again and the second speaker was introduced; a woman who identified herself as Sylvia said she was a drug addict and an alcoholic. She had been hospitalized after a failed suicide attempt. The psychiatrist at the mental institution where her family took her told her, "Nine times out of ten, when a person commits suicide, they're killing the wrong person."

Munch laughed at that. At the end of the meeting, they all held hands and said a prayer. It started, "Our Father, who art in heaven . . ." She recoiled in shock. Images flashed through her mind of Flower George lying there, stoned and naked, his glass eye staring at her, the other rheumy and oblivious; the gun, hot in her hand; the smell of gunpowder; her ears ringing. All these memories flashed through her head in an instant. She even felt the relief that had come over her, as if the bullets had purged something festering inside her. The woman holding her hand kept a firm grip, even gave her a little squeeze and mouthed to her, "It's okay." Munch watched the lips of the people around her and picked up the words as they uttered them. On the way to the stretch of leafy roadway shoulder she claimed as home, she threw away the syringes.

12

The next morning, Munch took her now-customary stool at the Denny's counter. It was Friday, payday. Ruby poured her a cup of coffee.

"I went to that meeting last night," Munch said.

"Did you like it?"

"What makes you think any of that stuff has to do with me? You've never seen me stoned, have you?"

Ruby snuck a quick glance up the counter, then pushed up the sleeve of her sweater. Munch could make out the faded blue scars running along the veins of her arm. "I know the signs. I've been there. I knew it the first second I saw you."

"So how do you get a sponsor?"

"Are you asking me?"

"That depends. What does a sponsor do, exactly?"

"I'd be happy to." Ruby pulled her sleeve back down and reached across the Formica counter to pat Munch's hand. "Here's how it works. I share my experience, strength, and hope with you. It keeps me clean and sober, too. We keep what we have by giving it away. All I ask is that you be honest with me. Can you do that?"

Munch looked away. There was always a catch.

"Listen," Ruby said, "don't tell me anything you're uncomfortable with. Trust takes time. It won't do you any good if you don't feel like you can trust me. We'll take it slow." She poured a second cup of coffee for herself. "There's another meeting at St. Anthony's tonight. Do you want to go?"

"I'll meet you there." She didn't want to be anywhere without her own set of wheels.

"I have to warn you—it's an AA meeting. If you identify yourself, say that you're an alcoholic, not an addict."

"Does your God care? There was a lot of God stuff in all the literature."

"Don't let the God stuff throw you. Call it a Higher Power, if that will help. Usually, an addict's 'God' needs the meeting more than the addict does."

"How can that be?"

"It's a Higher Power, as you understand Him. In a sense, you create Him to fit your needs."

"That doesn't make any sense. He is or he isn't. How helpful can he be if I'm supposed to make him up?"

"Oh, He's very real. You just have to reinvent your relationship with Him. I have to warn you—He has a sense of humor. He likes to throw the most unlikely angels at you."

"That, I can believe. So how come I gotta say I'm not an addict? Do you want me to lie?"

"Nooo." She drew the word out slowly. "It's just that druggies have such a poor success rate, people don't like to work with them. They break your heart. How many addicts were at the meeting you went to the other night?"

Munch did a quick calculation. "About thirty-five, I guess."

"The odds are that only two of the addicts in that room will stay clean."

Munch stirred her coffee and wondered who the other one was going to be.

"They say your emotional development is arrested when you start using," Ruby said. "It begins again when you get clean."

Munch reached for another slice of toast. If that were true, she'd be ten.

"I was reading about all the steps. The fourth one says something about making a complete moral inventory. Does it have to be written? I hate to put anything in writing, you know? Then I read the next step. It says I'm supposed to share it all with another human being. I don't know if I could do that."

"Whoa. You're getting kind of ahead of yourself. What about the first three steps? Admitting that you're powerless over drugs, that you need help from a power greater than yourself, and turning your will and life over to the care of that Higher Power?"

"I've done that."

"Oh." Ruby looked at her in surprise. "That's good." She looked at Munch again as if not sure what to say.

"The last time I was in jail."

"Jail's a good place for spiritual revelations," Ruby said.

"I was in Van Nuys for five days. It was Veterans Day weekend and I had a felony seventy-two-hour hold, so I ended up spending a long time there waiting to be transferred to Sybil Brand. After the second day, I asked them to transfer me to a solitary cell. I was tired of listening to all the broads bragging about what good whores they were. I mean, what does that mean? I know their bail had to be five hundred dollars. Where were their great pimps? I guess the ten percent bondsman's fee of fifty bucks was too steep for their man's budget. Such bullshit, you know?"

Ruby nodded.

"So anyhow, I'm there and I'm thinking, I need help. I'm about to turn twenty-one. I counted—this was my thirteenth arrest, only six of which they knew about. According to the public defender assigned to me, that six was plenty. I mean, I had already tried a lot of different stuff to straighten out my life. My best thinking always seemed to get me back to square one. I tried using only pills: uppers and downers. I tried just drink, but that just made me sloppy and I got in just as much trouble. Arrests number two and three were for drunk driving.

"I tried hanging out with the Satan's Pride, that was plan D. D for dumb, dangerous, and degrading. Bikers don't like junkies; no one does really. I thought that that would force me to stay clean, being around guys who would kick my ass for shooting up. They just ended up giving me that many more reasons to get oblivious. All my experimenting always led back to dope. So I figured I needed help from a source greater than myself. I even used those words in my head. The monster was too much to fight alone. Maybe, I figured, it was time to investigate this God thing; maybe there was some source of power out there that I could tap in to, to help me, like."

Ruby listened carefully, wiping the same spot on the counter.

"They feed you twice a day in Van Nuys. Breakfast is at six A.M.: French toast with some sort of reconstituted scrambled eggs served on an aluminum tray. The jailers don't come back until six in the evening, with Salisbury steak, lima beans, and bitter black coffee, if you wanted it. The only guard I saw other than the one who brought my meals was the female deputy who walked to the end of the corridor outside of my cell. Her job was to make notations on a clipboard every four hours after she checked to see that I was still breathing. Her timing seemed to coincide with whenever I managed to drift off to sleep. The cop would shout, 'Hey!' at me until I answered; then she would make a check mark on her chart and leave again.

"The next time the guard passed my cell, I spoke out. 'Got a minute?' I asked her. She said no, and I didn't blame her. You know, Van Nuys is only supposed to be a temporary holding facility. The criminals who come through there are usually drunk or loaded. They swear at the guards, get in fights, and by the next morning, they're usually gone. So I was really surprised when she turned around and came back. She asked me what was up and I told her.

"She listened to me and then told me to wait there, that she'd be right back. Like I could go anywhere. She brought back the desk sergeant and he was some kind of Holy Roller. He had me put my hands on the bars and pray with him. I mean, his eyes rolled back in his head and his voice got all singsongy. It was kind of embarrassing, but I went along with it because I knew they were just trying to be nice."

"So you felt different afterward?" Ruby asked.

"Well, it wasn't really what I had in mind. I thanked them both, and after they left, I just looked up and said, 'This is the way I see it. I've been bad and I need to pay. I'll do ninety days on the marks beef—that's only fair. When I get out, I'll stay clean. Just a few beers now and then. Is weed all right?' Then I remembered where I was, so I added, 'Lord, no weed, either.' That was the deal. Two hours later, the bus came to take me to Sybil Brand." Munch stirred her cold coffee and looked down. "Keeping up my end of the bargain was harder than I thought it would be."

Ruby grabbed Munch's hand and said, "I'll help you with your fourth step. Don't worry. You haven't done anything that anyone else hasn't done. The purpose of all this is to feel good about yourself, wipe the slate clean."

"I don't know. I've done some pretty bad shit."

"Everybody says that. Addiction does terrible things to people. It turns men into thieves, women into whores. One time, I—"

"I was never a whore," Munch said hotly, slapping her palm down suddenly on the counter. "Whores do it for nothing."

Ruby blushed. "Just keep going to meetings. You'll listen to everyone's story and discover that you haven't done anything or thought anything that's so unique."

Munch shrugged and got busy with the cream and sugar.

"Later, you'll make a list of all the persons you have harmed."

Here we go with the lists again, Munch thought. Everybody wants lists.

Ruby touched her cheek. "Be sure you put your name *first* on that list."

13

At 10:00 A.M., Lt. Mark Ladoor stopped St. John in the hallway. "It's my birthday," he said.

"Happy birthday. I didn't know."

"Don't worry about it. I'm just telling you because I want you to have lunch with me today."

Mace was flattered. He liked Mark Ladoor. Over the years, they had developed an excellent relationship, based on a mutual approval of each other's abilities to do their jobs. Mark Ladoor had come up through the ranks, distinguishing himself in the field. He had been shot in '72 while responding to a bank robbery. Mace would never forget the watch commander's emotional briefing following the shooting. An officer had been wounded, he said, and that was one too many. The bank robbers were tracked to a home in Culver City, near the projects on Bradford. They were given one chance to surrender; then the order was given to fire in the residence until the walls fell down. Neither suspect had survived and no other officer had been wounded.

Mark Ladoor returned to active duty six months later with a zipperlike scar that ran from his navel to his sternum and a promotion to sergeant. By '74, he had made lieutenant in the Robbery/Homicide division. He was liked as well as respected, due in large part to his policy of giving the detectives under him plenty of operating room, especially Mace, who had proven his judgment to be sound.

They agreed to meet at noon and Mace returned to the task at hand. He had pulled the boxes of field identification cards gathered in the last six months having to do with local bikers. He sorted through the large stack till he found what he was looking for. The files were cross-referenced by monikers. In recent years, the police had begun taking pictures to augment their files. He thought it was very cooperative of the bikers to give themselves such accurate identifying marks. The picture of the prospect in the bar revealed that the man had a distinctive tattoo on his right arm—a bushy black-and-white tail of a skunk that ran down his forearm. St. John flipped through his collection of Polaroids till he found a match. The biker's name was Jeffrey Roland Johnson, aka "Stinky." According to their information, he had passed initiation and become a full-fledged member of the Satan's Pride sometime in early February. Mace wrote this fact in his notebook.

He then put in a call to his old friend Bob Marshall at the DEA. They had gone through the Academy together in '68, when Mace got out of the service.

Bob was the lieutenant in charge of deep-cover operations at the DEA. They'd stayed in touch, held each other's chins up through their respective divorces. When Bob came to the phone, he sounded like his old self.

"How you doing, you old rattlesnake?" he asked, then launched into his first priority. "Getting laid?"

"Have to beat them off with a stick. How are the kids?"

"I see them on weekends. How's your dad?"

"He's hanging in there; you should come by the house. He'd love to see you, tell you some of his old lies. We've got a poker game on Friday nights."

"I don't know. Digger always seems to come up with four of a kind, and I've never been able to bluff you yet." Bob chuckled, then asked, "What's up?"

"I'm investigating a homicide. The Satan's Pride Motorcycle Club is involved. Do you have anybody on the inside?"

Bob whistled. "Those are some bad boys. Real closemouthed bunch. The charter members all served together in Nam, in the H Twenty-seven. Remember that?"

"Not really. I think I was in country when some kind of scandal broke. Some charges about unsanctioned executions, right? I never really heard the whole story."

"Nobody did. The lieutenant of the platoon was one Michael Lewis Sinclair, aka "Crazy Mike," current president of the Satan's Pride. The H Twenty-seven specialized in interrogation and special psyche ops: They ran clandestine missions, demoralizing the enemy by assassinating key figures in the Cong villages. Very black, covert stuff, a lot of deep in-country work with no support. The word is, it got out of hand. Your boy Sinclair got too good at what he did, went too far. Some of his methods offended Western sensitivities."

"We were out of our element there," St. John conceded. "The ROK Marines had a much better handle on the situation. We were still trying to win the natives over with nylons and chocolate bars. They'd play Korean roulette till someone felt like talking."

"Korean roulette?"

"A bullet in every chamber."

"Well, apparently Lieutenant Sinclair learned to adapt to the Indonesian mind-set and then some. According to our records, Michael Lewis Sinclair enlisted with his brother, Joseph Mark Sinclair. Joseph Mark didn't make it back."

"Killed in action?"

"Yeah, but not the kind of action you're thinking of. He got VD, some strain of incurable syphilis. The army had a standing policy of never sending a soldier home who'd contracted something we couldn't cure back home. In the sixties, they sure didn't want an epidemic of an incurable sexually transmitted disease to hit stateside. So instead, they transferred the poor son of a bitch from unit to unit till he died; then they burned his body and sent home his tags."

"I heard about that black syphilis. My ex works for the Health Department, social services."

"Then she can tell you how fast that kind of shit can spread. Anyhow, after Joseph died, Mike Sinclair went off. He took his unit into a hamlet and rounded up the women. I heard he played 'she loves me, she loves me not' with their fingers and toes. That was just a rumor, of course—noncorroborated. None of the boys in his unit ever broke down under questioning."

"If I remember right," Mace said, "the whole unit was discharged on a Section Eight."

"That's right," Bob said. "What you didn't know was that when they returned to the States, they formed a bike club."

Mace felt a chill spread through his bones. "I need to get close to this asshole, Bob. Are you running any kind of operation against him?"

"I am, but I don't want it getting fucked up. Your Crazy Mike is a slippery son of a bitch. Have you run a rap sheet on him?"

"Not yet."

"Don't bother. He's clean. I don't mean just no convictions. I mean no charges, no arrests, nothing. All we got on him is what the army supplied, and there's not much of that. Born and raised in Michigan, no surviving relatives, moved to California after he left the army in '71. No visible means of support other than his disability checks. I know he's dirty as hell; we've just never been able to get anything on him. He's crazy like a fox.

"I've got a man in deep cover. He's spent the last five years just being a biker, living the life. To be honest with you, I don't give a shit about your homicide. The Pride has a methamphetamine operation we've been trying to crack for three years. Crazy Mike's no fool. He plays it real careful before he lets anyone get near him. He doesn't use drugs, doesn't even drink. He sleeps with an M-16, never a woman. But what the hay, maybe we can help each other out."

"I'm going to bring in this guy Stinky for questioning."

"Wasn't he one of the Seven Dwarfs?"

"I'll be sure to ask him that." Mace lowered his voice. "Can you arrange to have your agent in custody by tomorrow?"

"I think so. I'll give you a call later."

"Bob? If anyone asks . . ."

"I'll say it's a social call."

"Thanks." Mace hung up and saw that his phone was blinking with another call on line two. It was the captain, Donald S. Divine. Behind his back, they called him "the Duck"; he tended to quack under pressure. Now he was squeaking in one of his typical apocalyptic rages.

"St. John, I just got a copy of the ballistics report from your Mancini homicide. Why didn't you pass it along to Parker Center? I don't want to hear about you withholding any pertinent information on an RHD investigation. It's their case now. Are we clear on that?"

"Yes, sir. I'm just a little behind on my paperwork right now."

"I understand you're still pursuing the Mancini homicide. Don't waste a lot of time on that. Your board is filling up." He was referring to the five-by-seven chalkboard that he had installed in the squad room as an incentive to the detectives. It was a tally of homicides that had occurred in Venice since the first of the year. The murders were listed chronologically, using the victim's last name, and broken into columns under the names of the investigating detectives. Unsolved murders were written in red chalk; a suspect in custody changed the color to green; only a conviction erased the name—a conviction or a change in venue. The Glassen murder had been a red question mark while the corpse remained unnamed. He could still make out the faint outlines on the board. There were a lot of things the board didn't take into account, but the board was all that the Duck was interested in.

"You're the boss," Mace told him.

"I'll take that as an affirmative."

Take it any way you want, Mace thought as he hung up the phone.

WHEN he arrived at the restaurant, Lieutenant Ladoor was already seated. Mace was surprised to see that the man had ordered a drink. He motioned for Mace to join him.

"How much time you got in?" the lieutenant asked without preamble.

"Eight, almost nine years. Why do you ask?"

"Are you doing the job you thought you would be doing?"

Mace wasn't sure how to answer. This was the kind of talk usually reserved for two in the morning, after a night of drinking. He wondered if this was the booze talking now, or perhaps Ladoor was going through that midlife thing.

"What do you mean?" he asked, playing it cautious.

"I mean, do you think you're making a difference? You keep busting the same assholes for the same thing; a couple of years later—months sometimes—they're back out on the street. You don't even get to do real police work anymore. You spend half your time writing paper. The DA's case is more important than catching the guy who did it. Catching the guy is just the beginning. Knowing in your gut that he's the one. It don't mean shit anymore. First they expect you to put together a packet of evidence and deliver it to the DA with a hundred and ten percent bulletproof case. Then, with some pencil pusher's approval, you can go back out and try to find the guy again." He paused to sip his drink, then fixed Mace with a penetrating look. "What do you want? What are your dreams? Weren't you and your dad going to take a trip, see the country in that train of yours?"

Mace was happy in the shift of the conversation. It was the second time in almost as many days that the same subject had come up. What he wanted and what he had to do were not always the same things. But if they were talking dreams . . . "There are stretches of track that go through the Rockies in Colorado," he told Ladoor, "through the Royal Gorge of the Arkansas River, that are so beautiful, they'd make you cry. Trout as big as tuna, clean water, totally untouched." He sipped his water. "I'll get there someday."

"That's why I wanted to talk to you. You can't always count on someday being there. Every year, before my birthday, I have my annual physical."

Mace stopped dead; the hair on the back of his neck pricked up and a cold chill ran down his spine. What did they call that? Someone walking over your grave. He waited for Ladoor to finish delivering his news.

"I'm dying, Mace. Cancer, it's in my liver. I've got six months."

"Mark, I . . ."

"Save it—there's nothing you can say. Think about what I said." They ordered lunch. "So how's your tag-team investigation going? I hear you're giving the boys at RHD a run for their money."

"Yeah, the Duck's been chewing my ass out for it, too."

"Donald's just running scared. He isn't getting any younger."

"It's not just that," Mace said, feeling like his problems were insignificant in light of what Mark Ladoor had just confided. "I feel like every time I make a discovery on the Glassen case that I'm covering ground that should have—I don't know. It's like there's no follow-up."

Ladoor nodded. "You had trouble with Ernie before. Remember that teenage girl at Venice High?"

Mace nodded. "Santos, Christina Santos. She took a four-story nosedive off the bleachers at the football field."

"As I remember, Ernie tried to convince the ME that the cause of death was suicide. The coroner didn't want to back him up. The girl was eight weeks pregnant. There were too many things that didn't add up."

"Her purse was never recovered for one thing," Mace said. "When I asked Ernie what he made of that, he didn't think it was important. 'Case closed,' he said. His actual words were, 'The bitch did it to herself.' "

"What can I say? The guy can be an asshole."

"I suggested we talk to her boyfriend. Ernie said the boyfriend had nothing to do with it. Like he'd already talked to the guy. Later, I discovered that Ernie never even identified the boyfriend, much less questioned him."

"Everyone gets lazy now and then," Ladoor said. "It's human nature."

"He gets paid to do the job."

"You used some pretty strong language in the report you filed," Ladoor said. "I seem to recall phrases like 'grossly incompetent' and 'unfounded assumptions,' pretty gutsy talk for a rookie detective."

Mace felt the color rise in his cheeks. "Hey, I was young, but I meant every word. Didn't exactly endear me to the brass, did it?"

"Fuck them," Mark said, and motioned to the waitress for a refill.

"You know, the patrolman who responded to the Santos call said he found one of her molars fifty-four feet from her body."

"Fifty-four feet?"

"Yeah, he said he paced it off while he was waiting for us."

"The boyfriend ending up confessing, right?"

"Yeah, after I found his married ass."

"You came out all right," Ladoor reminded him.

The brass had offered Mace his pick of assignments where openings were available. Vice, Mace felt, held too many temptations for a married man. Besides, he hadn't gone into law enforcement so that he could arrest victims. Narcotics involved distasteful undercover work. He had no desire to run around in dirty clothes with Vaseline in his hair and a wire around his chest. Homicide was the obvious choice—crimes against persons, that's where his heart was.

To make room on the squad, Potts was sent downtown to

RHD. Whatever lapse of attention to duty that had caused Ernie to slack on the Santos murder wasn't typical of his overall performance as an investigator. He had distinguished himself time and again with his almost uncanny insights. Personal connections notwithstanding, he deserved the promotion to downtown. It was just as well, Mace thought. He and Ernie's disagreements over the handling of the Santos homicide had caused a serious rift in their relationship.

Mace and Ladoor spent the rest of the hour reminiscing. Later, Mace couldn't remember what he'd eaten, only the offhand way that Mark Ladoor had announced, "I'm done," then laughed at his private joke when the busboy cleared their plates.

THE interrogation of Stinky on Friday afternoon went how St. John expected it to. He waved the evidence he had under the biker's nose.

"You were the last known person seen with this girl." St. John showed him the photograph. Stinky stonewalled. "We got hair fibers." He showed the biker a picture of the red panties.

"You don't like my hat?" Stinky said. "Sue me, pig."

"Get him out of here," Mace ordered, playing the frustrated cop. They could hold him seventy-two hours without charging him; then they would have to let him go. He was certain that Stinky could quote the laws of custody and evidence chapter and verse.

Stinky was put in the misdemeanor holding tank with the other arrestees du jour. On the cot next to him, another biker lolled and smoked a cigarette.

"Those pigs don't have nothing," the prone man said, scratching his chest. "If they ask you anything, just hold your mud."

"What you in for, bro?" Stinky asked.

"They think I robbed some bitch." The other biker stabbed out his cigarette against the block wall and flicked the butt into the stainless-steel toilet bolted to the wall. "I told them to kiss my ass. They can't prove nothing and I wasn't there. You hear what I'm saying?" He held out his hand. "Ugly Bud."

"Stinky," the biker answered, grabbing the other's hand high in the air in an arm wrestler's grip. "You got that midnight blue panhead, right? I've seen you at the rock shop in the canyon. Righteous sled."

"Right on, bro. You ride with the Pride, right? I hear you dudes throw some hellacious parties."

"I'll be out by Monday. Look me up; I usually hang at the Venture Inn."

"I'll do that, bro. Got a smoke?"

Mace and Cassiletti watched the performance through surveillance monitors.

"Looks like we're in," Mace said.

14

Her first paycheck went toward rent at a motel on Victory Boulevard that offered rooms by the week. A leering manager with a greasy ponytail showed her to her room on the second floor. He left her with towels and the reminder that he worked all night. She gave him a bored, uninterested look, then locked the dead bolt after him. The kitchenette consisted of a small, noisy refrigerator, a two-burner stove, and a Formica-covered table that attached to the wall. The last paint job had been poorly done. The motel had gotten a good price on the pumpkin-colored paint, no doubt. Dried teardrops ran from the corners of the walls and flecks of apricot peppered the brown industrial carpet. A cheap shiny yellow-and-red-flowered bedspread covered the twin bed against the opposite wall. The bathroom was the only part of the room with a separate door. Munch was delighted to discover that it even had a window that opened. All in all, she felt it was money well spent.

She unpacked her supplies on the counter of the small bathroom. Five dollars of her hard-earned cash had gone toward toothpaste, toothbrush, and shampoo. She spent half an hour in the shower, luxuriating in the feel of the hot water. She never knew how good soap could smell, or how bad it could feel to be dirty.

She dried her hair with the skimpy motel-provided towel, rubbing her scalp briskly till her hair stood out in damp light brown tufts. The scabs on her arms were finally showing signs of healing, and the angry red scars seemed to have toned down a shade. When she was using, she kept meaning to use the veins in her legs to spread the marks around so that there wasn't such a telltale concentration on her left arm. It never failed, though; when the time came, when she actually had the dope in hand, the anxiousness would overcome her. She'd say, "Fuck it" one more time and go for old reliable. Often she'd just lift up an old scab with the point of the needle and reenter the same hole, convincing herself that this was just as good as a leg shot because she wasn't really making a new mark.

The scarring was internal, as well. At least that's what she figured was happening when she felt the vein push aside, resisting the rape of the needle. More likely, the damn needle was just too dull, the steel point used a hundred times.

God, how she missed it—her habit. She felt like some huge part of her was missing, the foundation that she had built her life upon. It was her purpose, the thing that drove her; the disease that was killing her. How she craved the oblivion of sweet opium dreams, even the illusion of them. What a lying bastard the monster was. It had been a long time since getting down felt good. Shooting dope just felt better than not shooting dope. She had felt some strange, sick security in the predictability of it. Life was very simple when she was strung out; her existence was whittled down to the bare bones of need. Someone told her at one of the meetings that it was a long journey between learning not to die and learning how to live. This staying clean was like a new high in itself. Who would have thought that that would be the answer? To do no drugs at all. She had always believed that it was just a matter of getting the chemical combination right.

Tonight's meeting began at 8:30. She guessed she would go.

On her way to her car, she spotted a pay phone by the manager's office. She had time before she left for the meeting to give Wizard a call and let him know how she was.

Standing at the open booth, she tugged self-consciously at her new clothes. Ruby had gone through her closet and come up with a few new outfits for her. She presented them to her after work in a brown shopping bag from Hughes Market. At the bottom of the bag was a macramé purse with a strap made out of wooden beads. Munch tried to let it hang from her shoulder, as she had seen other women do, but it kept swinging out and banging into her back. It felt just as unnatural to clutch the purse in her hand. She tried strapping it across her chest, but then she was left with an arm that had nowhere to hang.

On the third ring, Wizard answered. "Venice Cab," he said.

"Hey," she said. "What's up?"

"You are, little one. All kinds of people been asking for you. You best just stay gone."

"I'm doing real good. I've been clean for six days."

"That's fine, real fine."

"Who was asking about me?"

"The Man was here. He gave me a message for you. He said he talked to your PO and would square everything. All he wanted, he said, was the piece and to know where you got it."

"What did you tell him?"

"I told him I hadn't seen you, didn't want to see you, and wished I'd never seen you. He left me his card."

"You said people. Who else?"

"Crazy Mike."

She felt her stomach clench. "What did that asshole want?"

"He said you done him dirty. He wanted to know where you were."

"What did you say?"

"I told him you was long gone."

"Should have told him I died." She studied the traffic driving by, all the good citizens going home. She watched the faces of the commuters, resigned to their wait. It must be nice to be bored,

126

she thought. She fought an impulse to wave at them. They were tired now, a good tired. They didn't know how good they had it. "Are you going to be there later?"

"I'll be here for a while yet. Don't do anything stupid. Don't mess things up for yourself."

Rush-hour traffic showed the first signs of dying down, and the speed began to pick up. A Cadillac darted into an opening too small for him—another commuter willing to die for ten feet of asphalt. The driver of the car he cut off honked his horn.

"I just want to square things," she said. "They never give up on murder. If I get the gun that they want so bad, I can bargain with it. They don't want me; they want the asshole I stole it from. I've never given anyone up before, but for that animal, I can make an exception."

After she hung up, she went back up to her room. Ruby had given her a coat, too. It was big on her and had deep, sagging pockets that fell open below her waist. She filled them now with her few belongings and left the purse on the bed.

EVANGELINE helped Mace spread the green felt cover over the dining room table. They brought in chairs from the den and placed them around the table in readiness for the night's game. Mace put Digger in charge of distributing the chips. Cassileti was invited, as was Bob Marshall from the DEA. The regulars would also be there: Mando Loyola from Records and Jimbo Washington from Vice. Evangeline set out bowls of chips and pretzels. Mace fitted a visor on his dad's head.

The traditional Friday-night game had begun ten years ago. They used to rotate houses, but now they usually met at Digger's. The old man was more comfortable in a familiar setting.

By seven o'clock, all the participants were seated. The buy-in was ten dollars. They had learned the necessity early on of setting a reasonable limit to keep the game friendly. Mace dealt first.

He called the game. "Baseball. Seven card stud, threes and nines wild, extra card on a four." The players anted.

"So when you going to go out with Carol?" Jimbo asked Mace. "You know she wants it."

"It's your bet," Mace said.

"Check," Jimbo said after lifting the two cards that were dealt to him facedown, then grimacing. "I'm serious. She's a fine-looking piece of woman."

"She's not my type," Mace said, and threw in a blue chip to see the bet on the table. He dealt another round of cards.

Bob Marshall snorted. "What the fuck are you talking about, 'type'?"

"Yeah, she's breathing and willing," Mando said, jumping in to the conversation. "That's all the type Bob ever needed."

"Look where it got him," Mace said. "Child support and a one-bedroom apartment in Culver City."

"I wouldn't talk, Engineer Bill." Bob raised the bet. "How much are you paying your ex?"

"C'mon, c'mon," Digger grumbled impatiently. "You gonna play, or you gonna yap?"

Mace laughed. "He must have a good hand. I fold." The rest of the players followed his lead. Digger turned over his cards. With the wild cards, he had a total of five eights. Mace helped him sweep his chips from the center of the table to the stack in front of him. It was Bob's deal.

"I'm serious," he said to Mace. "Ask her out. What's stopping you? You know she'll say yes."

"Don't laugh."

"Scout's honor."

"The truth?" Mace asked. At those magic words, all play stopped and the other men leaned forward in anticipation. "She bites her nails."

"Aww, man." The men exhaled in unison.

"With an ass like hers, I don't care if she bites her toenails." Jimbo seemed truly disappointed.

Mace shrugged. "C'mon, what's the game?"

"No peekee."

"So what's it like," Bob asked, "working with the Putz again?"

"Same old shit," Mace said. "He's not all bad."

"Who are you talking about?" Digger asked.

"Ernie Potts, Dad. You remember him. My old partner? Kind of a big guy, bald head, always wore those bow ties?"

"Whatever happened to him?" Digger asked. "He used to play with us."

"He got married, for one thing," Mace said.

"Yeah," Jimbo said. "Now every Friday night, he tells his wife not to wait up because he's got a game."

The men laughed.

"What's his wife like?" Cassiletti asked.

"She's real quiet, kind of jumpy," Mace answered. "I only met her a few times."

When it was Cassiletti's turn to deal, he called for a five-card draw. Guts to open. Mace opened with a two-dollar bet, which put everyone else out except Mando and Cassiletti. The betting raised until Cassiletti doubled. Mace threw his cards down in disgust. "You got it."

Mando folded on the same round.

"What did you have?" Bob asked.

"Nobody paid for that information?" Cassiletti said, and actually blushed as he collected his pot.

"Still waters run deep," Bob said, then laughed. "Hey, Mace, you don't think your bunkie here bluffed you, do you?"

"I guess we'll never know."

"Hey, where's the bathroom in this joint?" Digger asked.

The men seated around the table got busy with their chips.

"What are you talking about, Dad?" Mace stood up. "Quit joking. It's down the hall, where it's always been." He helped his dad up.

Digger pushed through the swinging door to the kitchen. Before it swung shut again, everyone heard him say to Evangeline, "This looks just like my house."

THE call came in at eight o'clock. Evangeline answered on the first ring and came in the dining room to tell Mace it was for him. Mace took it in the den. It was Dispatch. He was patched through to Jerry Parker, a detective on the night shift.

"What's up?" he asked. Through the open door, he could see Bob trying to convince Digger to stop turning his cards faceup. His dad was tired.

"We picked up a call at the cab company. I think your suspect is planning to pay a visit."

"Thanks, buddy. I'm on it." He hung up and rejoined the players in the dining room. "We've got to go in. Sorry, fellas."

"Great timing." Mando looked pointedly at the stack of chips in front of Mace's place.

Mace grinned, then motioned to his partner: "C'mon, Cassiletti, you can use the overtime."

Cassiletti asked to use the phone and then joined Mace outside.

WIZARD preferred to work nights under bright mercury floodlights. The business slowed down after ten. He used the uninterrupted time to patch together his mismatched fleet of taxis. A six-year-old Doberman named Bradly patrolled the perimeter beneath a battered chain-link fence, the top two feet of which were strung with razor wire. During the day, the two sliding gates that faced Brook and Main streets were left open so the cabs could move freely in and out. Once the sun went down, a heavy chain secured with a case-hardened padlock held the gates shut. Drivers radioed ahead when they were on their way back.

A dirt alley ran behind the shop and a graffiti-decorated

cinder-block wall separated the two. Broken beer bottles imbedded in the concrete on top of the wall discouraged unwanted visitors.

Munch parked the GTO in the alley and walked around to the front of the yard. The chain wasn't stretched all the way tight and the gate fit loosely in its track. The resulting slack allowed her to create a gap of five or six inches when she leaned into it. She slid through the opening and braced herself for the dog's attack. Bradley greeted her with both paws on her shoulders, pushing her against the fence. His joyful yelps brought Wizard around.

"Hey," she said.

"Hey, yourself. What are you doing here? I thought I told you to stay gone."

"The way I figure it, I got a chance to set things right. I don't want to be running for the rest of my life. I'm thinking I might call that cop."

He sighed wearily and shook his head in disgust. "Come inside," he said, "off the street." He led her into the office. It was little more than a storage room with a cage where he kept his radio equipment, paperwork, and spare parts. A naked lightbulb swung over his desk. The desk was built of milk crates and an old front door with knob and mail slot still attached. He used the doorknob to store rubber bands and centered his wastebasket under the mail slot.

He took a seat in his throne, a pivoting black vinyl desk chair worn to his shape and lovingly embalmed in silver duct tape. She sat opposite on a stack of tires with usable tread. Wordlessly, he unfastened the large round wristwatch that he always wore. Beneath it was a shiny mass of puckered scar tissue. "Do you know how I got this?" he asked her.

"I figured you burned yourself welding."

He shook his head and jabbed at the damaged flesh with a big black finger. "When I was a youngster, about your age, a man put a hundred-dollar bill on my arm here. He told me that if I could hold still till his cigar burned through that I could keep the hundred dollars." He held his wrist beneath her face so she could take a good look. "I learned a very important lesson."

"Did you get to keep the money?"

"No, I did not." He strapped his watch back on and wagged a finger at her. "What I learned was this, don't ever try to play a man at his own game."

"You don't have to worry about me. I'll be careful. You got that cop's card?"

Before she returned to her car, she stopped at the edge of the cinder-block wall that bordered the alley. The third cinder block from the end, up about three feet, was chipped at the top. She worked the mortar loose till she made an opening. She glanced up and down the alley once, saw no one, then slipped her hand inside. She winced as the tender skin on her wrists and forearms scraped on the rough plaster and scooted back the sleeve of her coat. She raised up on tiptoes and stretched taller, pushing her arm inside the opening all the way to her elbow. Something brushed against her fingertips, something soft and alive. She recoiled, but her arm stuck. She had never been squeamish before. This new sensibility must be another double-edged gift of sobriety, she thought, this acute awareness of everything icky.

She took a few deep breaths to steady herself. It's okay; it's okay, she chanted to herself. She repeated the prayer Father Frank had given her. When God is with you, who can be against you? There was another list she could make, she thought wryly.

She exhaled and closed her eyes, stretching her fingertips as far as they could reach. Sweat broke out on her back and forehead. She was rewarded by the feel of something smooth and cold, something steel. It was too far down in the blocks of the wall to get a grip on it. She worked her arm out of the opening, leaving skin and blood on the edges. When she at last worked her arm free, she held it against the outside of the wall to measure how far down the gun had dropped. She figured it had fallen right behind the black V in some gang member's spray-painted VENICE RULES. She picked up a rock and scratched a crude X. Then she replaced the mortar and returned to her car.

ACROSS Brooks Avenue, in the alley behind the houses there, a 1972 brown AMC Matador with Colorado plates and a Zig Zag man decal in the front windshield sat with the engine turned off. The detectives had been staked out there for the last three hours, ever since they received the call that their suspect might show up.

The two men watched her exploration of the wall with great interest.

"You get the girl," Mace told Cassiletti, "and I'll go see what's in the wall."

Cassiletti handed Mace the keys so that he could open the trunk. Mace tossed the keys back and retrieved a flashlight and a tire iron. He jumped when the siren blared into the quiet of the alley.

"What the fuck?" he yelled. "Cassiletti, what's the matter with you?"

Munch's head shot up and for a second her face was caught in the light.

"Grab her," Mace yelled, and the two men rushed toward her.

They heard her yell, "Bradly!" and the next thing they knew, a black apparition of snarling muscles leapt over the wall and joined them in the alley.

"Watch the dog," Mace said, but it was unnecessary. Cassiletti was already back in the Matador and grinding the starter. Mace pulled his gun. The Doberman growled and bared his teeth at the detective as he stepped backward. Mace aimed. The animal turned and leapt fluidly back over the wall.

Cassiletti pulled alongside Mace. "Sorry, Sarge. I hit the switch with my knee. You wanna try to find her?"

"Nah, she's gone." Mace burned a look at his partner. "Let's see what she was so interested in." Flashlight in hand, he carefully examined the wall, letting the beam play down to the childish X marking the spot.

"Looks like we still might get two for the price of one."

15

$\mathbb{M}$unch ran back to her car. Saliva kept filling her mouth and she spit it out. Her hands shook as she found the ignition switch with her key. Somehow, she managed to start the car and put it in gear.

She had lost them. She was pretty sure. If there were more of them, they would have stopped her by now. Brenda's house was two blocks away. The thought came to her innocently, disguised as mild curiosity: Was Brenda holding? It would be so easy to stop.

Just as it occurred to Munch that she had a pocketful of money, red flashing lights filled the rearview mirror of the Pontiac. It was an all-too-familiar sight. A sickening deposit of acid collected in her stomach and quickly spread to the back of her throat. She pulled the car over and watched in her side mirror as the cop approached. She knew to make no sudden moves. His hand rested on the butt of his pistol as he swaggered toward her.

"Step out of the car, please," the cop said. "Nice and easy. Keep your hands where I can see them."

"What's this all about, Officer?" she asked, wide-eyed, "I wasn't speeding, was I?"

"I'll need to see your license and registration." He swept the beam of his light through the interior of her car and then back in her eyes.

She graced him with a quirky little smile and complied.

"Wait here," he said. He retreated back to his cage car with her temporary license in his hand.

A million "would haves," "could have," and "if I'd only's" coursed through her mind in a matter of a few adrenaline-charged seconds. Her brain hit turbospeed as her hands clenched the top of her open door. A number of alternate choices she might have made filled her head. Her eyes shifted between watching the cop in her side mirror and stealing quick glances at the ignition key dangling from the switch in the dash.

She struggled to keep calm as a litany of indecipherable clipped sentences and numbered codes passed between the cop and the static-charged voice coming back over his radio. She watched the cops expression but couldn't read it.

The cop glanced up as a car passed with its radio turned up to full volume. She smiled at him and he went back to reading the numbers on her registration into his microphone.

She started to get angry. Why couldn't they just leave her alone? The cop looked up and she glared at him. His eyes narrowed back.

Jail, she was going to jail again. The memories of her last incarceration filled her.

She remembered how dark it had been when she'd first arrived at Sybil Brand. It had seemed to be morning, but she wasn't sure. Her days of incarceration in Van Nuys had left her disoriented.

They led her into a cold, windowless room, with three female prison guards watching closely from behind thick Plexiglas. Munch was told to undress.

"Everything off, ladies," the matron had said, bored and speaking into a microphone. The mechanical voice echoed off the stone walls.

The prisoner next to her pulled down her jeans, revealing men's boxer shorts.

"We got one for the Daddy tank," the guard announced.

"What's a Daddy tank?" Munch asked the black woman next to her.

"Shut your face," the woman answered.

"No talking, ladies," the guard said.

Munch was led into a second room. The floor was wet and cold under her bare feet. Two female guards waited till six naked prisoners were in the room before shutting the door. The seated deputy told them all to bend forward and spread open their cheeks and vaginas. Munch focused her attention on the six-inch grated drain in the center of the floor. When the officer was satisfied, the second one stepped forth with a tank and spray nozzle. She wore goggles and a mask, so Munch couldn't see her eyes as she sprayed her down.

"What's this?" she asked.

"Delousing spray," the faceless uniform answered. "No talking, eyes straight ahead."

They were led to another room, where they were issued light blue smocks, navy blue sweaters, and white rubber flip-flops.

"What size shoe you wear?" the girl behind the shoe bin asked. A badge clipped on her blue smock read TRUSTEE.

"Six," Munch answered.

The trustee handed her a pair of size eights. The prisoner behind her shoved her along. She shuffled her feet so that the shoes would stay on.

It was then the fear caught up to her. It seized her in icy arms and whispered in her ear, You're alone. It was the voice that had ruled her for the last seven years. It was the monster. It was not the guards she feared, nor the other prisoners. Her horror stemmed from the fear of facing the day with no chemical inside her.

The next part of the processing had involved a cursory medical examination. She told the nurse that she was an epileptic, a trick an old hype had taught her. She was issued a yellow armband that signified a special medical condition and entitled her to a twice-a-day call to the infirmary line. There, they gave her an assortment of tablets and capsules in a tiny white paper cup. They always made sure she took them all, made her open her mouth wide and lift up her tongue. No saving them up, they warned. The drugs weren't much, but at least it was something. After a week, the nurse told her that they were going to start reducing her medication. At lunch that day, in full view of everyone from cell block E, she faked a seizure, and there was no more talk of reducing her medication.

Her strongest memories of Sybil's Stroll were of the noise—the cacophony of voices echoing off the cement floors and walls; the colored girls screaming over their games of crazy eights in the dayroom; the fights over which soap opera to watch on the black-and-white TV mounted high on the wall and controlled by the guard in her booth; the solid thunk of steel bars sliding closed.

Three times a day, the inmates lined up in the hallway to be marched to meals. They weren't allowed to go till quiet was achieved. The guards were prepared to wait as long as necessary, so three times a day there was a break in the screaming. The whap of the rubber shoes in the hallway was the only noise permitted. The women made a game of slapping their shoes as loudly as possible. Munch had closed her eyes and pretended they were the sounds of horses on a cobblestone road.

The cop was through with his business. She watched him throw his silver clipboard back onto his passenger seat and walk back to where she waited.

At Sybil Brand, she had read a book a day—mysteries, Westerns, romances, whatever was available on the cart. That part wasn't so bad. The books had taken her to other worlds. She broadened her vocabulary as well, learned new adjectives, nouns, and verbs that didn't begin with the letter *f*. When she came upon a word she wasn't familiar with, she could usually figure out the meaning by the context of the sentence. There was so much more to life than the narrow world of shooting galleries and mirrored motel ceilings.

"You better roll your windows up," the cop said, bringing her back to her present situation and immediate problems.

Her shoulders slumped and she put her hands behind her back. Maybe he would let her leave the car for Wizard. She started to say something, but the cop spoke first.

"You were driving down an alley with your headlights off," he said as he returned her license and registration. "That's why I stopped you, Miss Signman. This is a bad neighborhood."

She didn't hesitate. "Thank you, Officer. Don't worry. I'm leaving."

16

I can't believe we missed her," Mace told Caroline. It was Saturday morning and he called her at home after getting her number from a clerk he knew in Santa Monica. "We were so close."

"What happened?"

"Our siren went off accidentally. It happens."

"Sure it does."

He could sense her smiling on the other end of the line, but he made no effort to clear up her misassumption as to how the girl had eluded them.

"Well, it wasn't a total loss," she said. "You retrieved the weapon."

"It won't do me much good if I can't link it to a suspect. It was wiped clean." He took a breath. "I was wondering if you had plans tonight? Maybe catch a movie, have dinner?"

"I'd like that," she said.

Mace remembered to breathe. "I'll pick you up at six. Where do you live?"

"You're the detective." She laughed then, a pleasant tinkling of fine crystal. "I'm sure you'll figure it out."

Mace looked at the paper in his hand. He even knew when she got her last parking ticket. "I'll see you then."

*　*　*

THE restaurant he took her to was in downtown L.A. It was a former dried-bean warehouse that had been converted to a restaurant and bar. It had been built during World War II next to the railroad tracks by a consortium of farmers to store their product. The silos where the beans and grains had been kept were painted Tuscan red and THE DEPOT was painted in Pullman green. The main attraction of the restaurant was the commuter train that passed by every twenty minutes. Over the bar, a bell sounded when the train was due, and those so inclined rushed to the open doors and waved at the passing locomotive.

Over an appetizer of salsa and chips, Mace and Caroline maneuvered through each other's histories, searching for points in common. They determined that they were both natives. She grew up in Santa Monica, he in Venice.

"How did you get into probation work?" he asked.

"From the other side of the desk." She sipped her margarita. "I ran with a rough crowd when I was a teenager. By the time I was seventeen, I had managed to pick up a few charges on my record."

He raised an eyebrow. "Such as?"

"Nothing too serious." She sipped her drink and he let the question go unanswered. "I got lucky. I was assigned a probation officer who cared. She took the time to convince me of the error of my ways, found me a summer job, got me involved in sports. She offered me a deal. If I could stay out of trouble for a year, she would seal my record."

"It obviously worked." He nodded thoughtfully. "So now you want to return the favor, give back to society."

If she caught the edge in his voice, her manner didn't betray it. "What about you, Detective St. John? Did you raise some hell in your youth?"

"Nah, I was a regular choirboy. My dad saw to that. He always kept me busy with summer jobs. Any time left in between school and work was devoted to training. I wanted to be a world-champion boxer."

"Aren't you kind of, um, small for a boxer?" She blushed as soon as the words left her mouth. He thought it was the most endearing thing he'd ever seen.

"Not for a middleweight," he explained.

"So why didn't you pursue it?"

"I was a bleeder. The refs kept calling the fights because they thought I was hurt. I tried soaking my face in brine, all kinds of things. Nothing seemed to help; I was just prone to cut. After high school, I joined the army. I liked the military, but two tours of the jungle cured me of those aspirations. I came back home, got married, went to the Academy, made detective, got unmarried."

"How long have you been divorced?"

"Two years."

"Do you still see her?"

"We keep in touch. I have to know where to send the checks." He tried to keep his tone light, but bitterness seeped through. Caroline studied the chip basket. "What about you?" he asked. "Ever been married?"

"No. I'd like to someday. I want to be really sure when I do. I only plan to do it once." She searched his face. "Your dad means a lot to you, doesn't he?"

"Sure. He raised me. When I got out of the service, we were going to see the country together. I got married instead." He shook his head. "I should have gone when we had the chance."

"You could still go, couldn't you?"

"Digger's not up to traveling much these days."

"Is he sick?"

"Not really. His heart is strong. He had a circulation problem a while ago, but surgery fixed that. His arteries were all clogged. The doctors said he was a walking time bomb. They always say that. When they operated, they said it looked like he might already have had a few silent strokes. The doctor said we should do a CAT scan. Nan—that's my ex-wife—explained that the scan would show how much brain damage there had been. What good would that do? It's not like you could cure it or anything. Brain damage is irreversible. I took Digger home after a couple of days. The doctor said I should look into a convalescent home, that Digger wasn't able to care for himself. He also said that pneumonia could be an old man's best friend."

Caroline's eyes filled with tears and she placed her hand on his.

"Have you ever seen those places?" he asked her. "They're like warehouses. I couldn't do that to him. Besides, he does all right. Don't kid yourself—he's sharp when he wants to be."

"How long did the doctor say he would live?"

"Probably another twenty years." Mace wiped salsa from his mouth. "If I'm lucky." He signaled the waitress. "Enough of this. I'm sorry I burned your ears off. Let's get something to eat."

Caroline nodded.

"I thought you said you didn't date cops," he said after they had ordered.

"The full quote is, 'I don't date someone just because they're a cop.' I date the man."

She fixed him with a searing look. At least that was the effect it had on him. Those blue-gray eyes of hers seemed to burn right through to his innermost self. Her intensity dried up his throat and made his heart thump. It was as if she discarded all the bull-shit on the surface and got right to his core. He found again that the challenge in those eyes was one he wasn't up to.

He tried to remember what she'd said. He needed to shift the conversation back to a verbal level. Something about not dating cops just because they were cops. He knew the phenomenon she was referring to. He had first encountered it in the service. Girls who never looked at him twice began falling all over themselves to go out with him. It happened right before he shipped out, after boot camp, when he had come home on leave. Digger told him it was the uniform. The new popularity pleased the other guys, but it left Mace strangely empty—a feeling he had always kept to himself. The transition to instant sex symbol didn't stop when he left the service. Whatever successes he'd had in dating tripled when he joined the police force. The ugliest guy in the world could put on the badge, it seemed, and get laid. Sometimes he wondered if that should somehow be incorporated into recruitment literature.

He realized that Caroline was different. But before he let her peel through his inner layers, he'd have to know a lot more about her.

After dinner, they stopped for a drink at a small bar in the marina that had pool tables and live music. The musician was a longhair who alternated playing an acoustical guitar and chromatic harmonica while singing sixties folk songs.

"Do you play?" he asked Caroline, gesturing to the empty pool table.

"A little," she said.

The second time she ran the table, Mace decided the woman had a gift for understatement, and he made a mental note to look up her juvenile record.

ON Sunday, Mace took a ride out to Playa del Rey. An old boyfriend of Vicky Glassen's had agreed to meet with him. Mace assured the boy that anything he said would be off the record. They met at a hamburger stand with a view of the ocean. They ordered cheeseburgers and french fries and found an empty table on the patio.

Mace let the boy choose his words.

"Vicky was a great gal," the boy said.

Mace nodded and threw a piece of his bun to a seagull, who snatched it up quickly.

"Real pretty, real smart."

"How long did you two go together?" Mace asked. The seagull invited a few of his friends and now five of the big white birds sat on the railing. Mace threw them french fries.

"A year and a half."

"Who broke it off?" The birds grew bolder. They hopped to the table next to the men and made demanding noises. Mace tried to shoo them away.

"I did."

"Why?"

The boy fidgeted.

"Don't worry. You can trust me." He watched while the boy came to what looked like a difficult mental crossroad, torn between speaking ill of the dead and telling the whole truth. There was a tenseness in his face. His chest filled with a deep breath that he held for some seconds. Mace held his own breath and sat perfectly still, recognizing the fragile moment. With a slight nod, the boy exhaled. His eyes closed slightly and his shoulders slumped. End of conflict; decision made. Mace leaned closer to catch every word.

"She started getting too . . . kinky."

"Kinky?" Mace asked quietly. A bird walked over and pecked at the tassel on his loafer.

"She wanted me to do things to her. Like when we were, you know, doing it."

"What kind of things?" He kicked lightly at the bird. It flapped its wings but made no effort to fly away.

"First, she just liked it when I talked dirty. More than just dirty, degrading. She told me to call her a bitch and a whore. Then that wasn't enough. She wanted me to slap her breasts and spank her. It was getting too weird. I couldn't get into it, so I broke it off."

"Was she upset when you did?"

"I think not," he said. "She just kind of laughed at me and said that was fine with her. I think she was already seeing somebody else."

"Somebody else?"

"The week she died, she gave me a little going-away present."

"What was that?"

"A dose of clap. Not just any clap, some new strain that's resistant to penicillin."

17

Munch went over to Ruby's apartment on Sunday afternoon to begin her fourth-step inventory. Ruby's apartment was in Sherman Oaks, north of Ventura Boulevard, the street that divided the socioeconomic borders of the San Fernando Valley neighborhood. The million-dollar homes on the hills that overlooked the valley were south of the boulevard. The people who worked in the service industries lived in the smaller, older homes and apartments to the north. Ruby's building was a typical example of sixties architecture, a boring stucco structure of straight lines and indented balconies. The landscaping consisted of close-cut squares of lawn and box hedges, but it was well maintained, if uninspired. They sat in her living room on an old sofa full of cat hair. Ruby set out a plate of cookies and a pitcher of lemonade. She apologized as two tabbies repeatedly rubbed themselves against Munch's legs.

"I don't mind," she assured her sponsor. The truth was, it was kind of flattering to have the animals take to her so. A fat tabby settled in her lap and she stroked its head till it purred as loudly as the air-conditioning unit buzzing in the window. "Where do we start?"

"Tell me about your childhood."

She ruffled the cat's ears and it playfully chewed on her fingers. "My mom was a beatnik. I remember that she had lots of hair; it always seemed to be covering her eyes, her face. She had a beautiful voice, kind of deep and trembling, like she was almost singing. We used to stay up late. I can remember the magic of the world after midnight. I'd be the only kid in a world of adults. Smoking, talking, they always seemed to be doing important things."

"Why do you think that?"

"I guess because I never understood what they were talking about and they always seemed to be taking one another so seriously." The cat stood up and stretched, arching his back and straightening out his tail. Wisps of marmelade-colored hair drifted lazily upward and were caught in shafts of light from the partially open venetian blinds. "We used to go to Sunset Strip, where the coffeehouses were. She liked musicians. I remember going to jazz sessions held in people's garages. We'd sit around on milk crates set up on concrete floors while the drummers and horn blowers played their riffs. I think she wanted to sing but lacked the courage. She used to sing for me, but never around other people. I remember she never learned how to drive."

"How did that make you feel?"

"I didn't like it. We always seemed to be at other people's mercy. Sometimes they'd take us places we didn't want to go. She wouldn't even remember the next day how we got there or what she had done. I hated it when she wouldn't remember, like she was doing it on purpose. She'd always be sorry—sorry and crying, face black with mascara and eyeliner." Munch stopped, surprised at her anger.

"Sounds like she might have been one of us," Ruby said gently. "Do you think she was an alcoholic?"

"She was also an addict. Totally. Heroin, mostly, pills, crank, but she drank some, too. And, of course, everyone was smoking pot. It wasn't like she didn't try to change. Toward the end, she kept trying to save herself with the Lord. Every Sunday, she'd drag me to church. The rest of the week, she got loaded. When I was eight, she OD'd. We were staying at some musician's house in Venice. When she wouldn't wake up, the guy freaked. He was afraid he'd get busted."

"What about your father?" Ruby asked.

"Let me work up to that."

"What about your mother's family?"

"They disowned her when she was a teenager. I never met any of them."

"So what happened to you when your mother died?"

"Flower George took me in. He said he was my father; it gave him legal guardianship and a monthly check. He also needed it to enroll me in public school, and later when he took me out."

"Was he good to you?"

"He pretty much left me alone till I was thirteen. Then I started growing tits, and I guess he remembered I was a female. He started saying that maybe he wasn't my father after all."

"Are you saying he molested you?"

Munch shrugged. "I guess you could call it that."

"When did he take you out of school?"

"When I was in the ninth grade. I remember I was mad about that—I liked school. George knew we could make more money on the street. That's when I started using dope. I always smoked weed, but never the needle before that. George gave me dope to reward me."

"That's awful."

"Well, he was an addict, too. So I guess we can't hold it against him."

"I'm not that forgiving. You're my friend, and he did you very wrong. The son of a bitch should burn in hell," Ruby said. She stood up in her anger, and the cats, sensing trouble, yowled and ran from the room.

"I'm getting to that part," Munch assured her, and reached for another cookie.

18

⊕n Sunday afternoon, Mace picked up a diagnostic psychiatric manual that Dr. Miller had recommended. He returned to the Bella Donna and fixed himself a can of chili, which he ate right out of the pot. When he finished eating, he settled into his high-backed wing chair and began to read. It was a pleasant evening; the Santa Anas were blowing a warm breeze off the desert. He left the door that opened to the platform open and propped his feet up on the chair's matching red Spanish-leather ottoman. The first thing he looked up was sexual sadism.

"The sadist," it said, "derives pleasure from inflicting pain and/or humiliation on his victim. The age at onset of sadistic tendencies varies but is usually chronic after the condition has presented. When practiced with nonconsenting partners, the activity is likely to be repeated until the sadist is apprehended. The severity of sadistic acts tends to increase over time and, when combined with antisocial personality disorder, may lead to serious injury or death of his victim."

The sun began its descent and took with it its light. Mace turned to the brass lamp beside his table and switched it on. His .38 rested beside him. The Tiffany shade cast soft spots of color on the ceiling.

Nan had called him paranoid when they were going through the divorce. The book had a small section on that. It was under the "Personality Change" section. "Diagnosis of this condition," it said, "is reached when the subject's predominant feature is sus-piciousness or paranoid ideation." Mace shook his head and snorted. He was a detective; of course he was suspicious. People did nothing but lie to him all day long. Just the same, he couldn't help but sneak a guilty glance at his service revolver, a graceless, repulsive weapon, devoid of color, devoid of warmth. Its dull black barrel and handle weren't softened by the glow of dusk. He opened the drawer of the lamp table and swept the weapon out of sight.

A moth had come in through the back door and was throw-ing itself at the bulb of the lamp. It ricocheted off the inside of the shade. There was no moon and the night came quickly. The blackness of outdoors seemed to increase the intensity of the light within the Bella Donna. The moths's frantic dance inside the lamp cast frenetic shadows against the window shades. He read on.

The section on sexual masochism read like the mirror image of sexual sadism. It described a sexual masochist as an individual who derives his sexual pleasure by being made to suffer. "This in-cludes fantasies of rape," it stated, "while being held or bound, with no possibility of escape."

He shifted uncomfortably in his chair, remembering enact-ments he had staged with an old girlfriend. She had asked him to use his cuffs. He had played along, even gotten a thrill from the total power he had felt over her. Idly, he wondered what it would have felt like if the woman had been unwilling. The moth fell to the table next to him, stunned and singed. He finished the paragraph.

"Sexual Masochists," the section concluded, "often increase the severity of their acts. The consequence is that over time, their actions could result in injury, or even death."

The moth regained consciousness and flew drunkenly upward for a final assault at the light. Mace flipped off the switch and closed the book.

His phone rang.

"Mr. Mace?" Evangeline sounded breathless. "Mr. Digger is lost again, I think."

He told her that he would be right over. In minutes, the Bella Donna was locked tight and he was out the door. It wasn't the first time Digger had wandered off and been unable to find his way home. Fortunately, he was well known in the community. The few times before, he had been recognized and helped home. Of course, that had been when it was broad daylight, not on a moonless night, when all manner of predators roamed the streets.

Mace cursed himself for not getting the ID bracelet the doctors had suggested. To tag his dad thus had seemed so undignified. He'd rejected the idea immediately. He couldn't feature his dad with a tag saying, "My name is Digger; if found, please return me." The guy was a war hero, not some German shepherd. Now he was lost and wandering the alleys of Venice, because Mace was too stupid to accept the truth, too caught up in his ideas of fucking dignity. He fought mental images of his dad, beaten and bloody, lying facedown in his own blood. He'd seen it too many times—victims stabbed for their wristwatches. Digger always wore a big gold Citizen. Mace beat his hand against his steering wheel and cursed himself as he raced toward Venice.

Ten minutes later, he arrived at the house on Carroll Canal. Evangeline met him at the door. She'd been crying. "Mr. Mace, he said he was getting the paper. He never came back. I called his name. The lady at the end of the block thinks she saw him walking that way." She pointed north, toward the gym, toward Ghost Town.

"What's he wearing?"

"Those pants you hate, the red ones. He wouldn't let me throw them away. He kept digging them out of the trash."

He squeezed her shoulder. "That's all right. That's good. He'll

152

be easier to spot." He didn't add that a white-haired white man wandering the streets of Ghost Town was already going to stick out like the proverbial snowball in hell, with about the same chances of survival. Mace called Dispatch and asked them to keep an eye out; then he hopped back in his car and headed toward the direction where Digger had last been seen.

He thought about the time when he was a kid and Digger had taken him to the La Brea tar pits. They had seen a cottontail caught in the oozing mire. Mace had wanted to scale the chain-link fence to save the little bunny. Digger had stopped him, saying that the rabbit was too far gone. "Look at his eyes, son," Digger said. "He knows he's done." Indeed, the rabbit eyes were blank and glazed; the animal clearly was resigned to his fate, sunk into shock, and had already begun to die. Mace had refused to leave. He had watched till all that was visible was the little white ball of its tail.

He now crossed Venice Boulevard and made a swing around the loop at the beginning of Main Street, the old Windward Lagoon. The winos on the steps of the post office didn't remember seeing anyone matching Digger's description. Mace continued down Main, past the park known as "Hooker Hill," which faced the elementary school.

He passed the bus station and slowed down when reached the row of houses on the other side of its parking lot. He spotted an elderly couple. They were sitting on their stoop in mismatched chairs, enjoying the respite from the winter chill. The man, a thin black skeleton in a threadbare T-shirt and old uniform pants, sat with his wife, a heavy woman in a bright yellow muumuu. They looked as if they had been there awhile. He called to them, but they refused to acknowledge him. They just stared vacantly ahead. He gave up.

He spotted another woman halfway down the block. She was watering down her yard. She tugged on the hose attached to her whirlybird. As the sprinkler scooted across the grass, it fell to one side. She righted it with an expert flick of her wrist, making the hose jump like a lariat. He rolled down his window and yelled to her.

"Have you seen a white man? Five eleven, a hundred and sixty pounds, red pants?"

The woman shook her head and looked down till he rolled past. He knew she probably didn't want her neighbors seeing her talk to the police. The people in that neighborhood could spot an officer of the law a mile away, off duty or not. Mace continued to cruise. When he got to Brooks, he turned right. The free clinic where Nan volunteered a day of her time a week was on the corner of Brooks and Main. Now it was closed and locked up tight. All the homes and businesses in the area were sealed with burglar bars. Every flat surface was marked with gang writing and the wounds of past gunfire. He wound in and out of the alleys and streets, wishing he had a searchlight. On the corner of Seventh and Sunset, he spotted them.

A skinny black kid held Digger's hand and was leading him to a car.

Mace honked and stepped on the accelerator. "Dad, Dad," he yelled. The two men looked at him and waited till he pulled up alongside.

"Hey, Officer St. John," the young black kid said. "Is this your dad? I was fixin' to bring him to the hospital. He's like confused or something."

Mace immediately recognized the kid. He was a local gang member, a Blood. They'd crossed paths professionally a few times. "Thanks, uh . . ." He tried to think of the kid's name; it was the least he could do—give him that recognition. The kid called himself something like Sleepy Dog, or maybe it was Fang. Mace couldn't bring the moniker to mind. He made a note to himself to look it up. "You were helping him?"

"Hey, I got a daddy, too," the kid said.

Mace looped a protective hand under his dad's arm. "He'll be all right. You just got lost, right, Dad?"

Digger stared at him. For an awful moment, it seemed as if he didn't recognize Mace. Then he spoke. "I can't remember where I parked my car."

"C'mon, Dad, I'll take you home." Mace turned to the kid and shook his hand. "Thanks again."

"He's a good man." Digger nodded toward his rescuer. "Give him a fin."

"I'll take care of him. Watch your head."

As he got in the car, Digger turned to Mace. "By the way," he said, "what's your mother making for dinner?"

Mace's heart dropped, but he forced a smile. "Let's go find out," he said, putting the car in gear.

19

On Monday morning, Mace called a company that made home-monitoring alarm wristbands. They were used primarily for prisoners under house arrest. They attached to the wrist or ankle and sent out a signal. When the prisoner left his home, he could be tracked. Even at an officer's discount, the device cost one hundred dollars a month.

He had just hung up from making the arrangements when a call came in. There had been a possible homicide in the Hampton Apartment complex. He strapped on his revolver and gestured for Cassiletti to join him. On their way out of the squad room, they passed under the infamous board. For the first time in two years, Mace had more unsolved cases then solved. It couldn't happen at a worse time. At roll call, it was announced that a lieutenant's position would soon be opening up in the precinct. Ladoor hadn't told anyone else about his illness, just that he was taking an early retirement. The sharks were already circling.

Mace added his name to the list for consideration. Another stripe would make a big difference for him. It would mean a pay hike, for starters. Between taking care of his dad, alimony, and his own expenses, his sergeant's pay no longer cracked his nut. An administrative position would also get him off the street. The red chalk on the board stared back at him.

What the board didn't say was that the double homicide last week was a drug murder, the most difficult to solve. An execution performed by some anonymous, emotionally uninvolved professional over a few hundred dollars' worth of powder. No witnesses, no evidence, no hope unless someone came forward and volunteered information. The solutions of those cases were a waiting game. Eventually, someone would talk. A bad guy would get busted and want to cut a deal, or someone's girlfriend would get mad and want to get even. But until the cards played out, the red chalk would remain.

The Mancini homicide was close to going down. His experience was that the wait would be short; the girl would trip herself. She would surface soon, to score some drugs or pick up some quick money turning a trick. But there was no color for "almost," and he wasn't making excuses.

Now with this new call, one more name would be added to the crowd of names on the board, keeping him that much further from promotion. He prayed that it would turn out to be a suicide.

"What have we got?" Cassiletti asked as he joined him in the hallway.

"Sounds like a domestic. Uniforms responded to a 'shots fired' call. They got a woman down. Paramedics took her to Marina Mercy, but they said it looked bad."

The drive to the Hampton Apartment Complex took twenty minutes in the Monday-morning traffic. The uniforms were standing by, having cordoned off the crime scene. Mace stepped under the yellow tape and surveyed the carnage. Still-moist blood spattered on the wall indicated a high-velocity impact. The wound inflicted on the victim had been made by a bullet, rather than by a knife or blunt instrument. He could see the outline on the carpet where the body had been found, a clean spot amid the blood. The gun lay nearby. The uniforms had left it undisturbed. They told the detectives that it lay exactly where they'd found it, near the woman's right hand.

"Suicide?" Cassiletti asked.

"No, I'm afraid not. The location of the gun is all wrong." Mace told the officers to get the names of all the neighbors who heard or saw anything. He turned back to his partner and said, "I'm going to call the hospital."

He used the next-door neighbor's phone while the crime-scene technicians lifted prints in the apartment. The nurse on duty in the emergency room at Marina Mercy informed him that the woman was DOA, ASTW—dead on arrival and stayed that way. St. John smiled to himself. Was it any wonder that so many cops dated ER nurses? They had the same twisted sense of humor. Normal people didn't understand. He caught himself. Normal people, as in people other than me.

"I'm on my way," he said.

"She'll be waiting," the nurse said.

He returned to the death scene at the woman's apartment.

"I'm going to the hospital," he informed the policemen who had first responded to the call and whose duty it now was to protect the crime scene. "Don't let anyone in here."

In the morgue of the hospital, Mace stared down at the mortal remains of Hillary Marks. She had been a woman of no outstanding beauty. The picture on her driver's license, which he had brought with him, showed a face with a stern, disapproving look. Death had not improved her. Her brown eyes stared blankly; her thin unpainted lips were open in an O-shaped expression of surprise; a hole gaped where her nose had been. He removed the bags around her hands and looked for gunshot residue. There was a wedding band on her left hand, a plain gold ring. Had she had children? He didn't even know. He turned over the palm of her right hand and noted the spatter. If she had been holding a gun, her palm would have been shielded from the spatter. He envisioned the name of "Marks, Hillary" appearing in red on the board.

"I'm going back to the apartment," he told the nurse. "I'll call the coroner to send a car."

He arrived back at the apartment to the sound of the phone

ringing. He nodded for the officer to pick up the extension in the kitchen.

"It's for you, sir," the patrolman said. "He asked to speak to the detective investigating."

Mace took the receiver and said, "This is Sergeant St. John."

"My name is Howard Marks," the caller said. "I killed my wife and I'd like to surrender to you."

"Hold on a minute." St. John cupped his hand over the mouthpiece. "We got a name of the victim's husband?"

Cassiletti consulted his notepad, "Howard Marks."

St. John nodded and returned to the call. "Where are you?"

"I'm calling from a pay phone. Shall I meet you at the station?"

"That would be great." He hung up. "I'm going back to HQ."

Two hours later, after being read his rights, Howard Marks initialed every page of his detailed confession and assured the detectives that he had done a terrible thing and should be punished for his crime. Another detective in contention for the lieutenant's position sat in on the interrogation, such as it was. As Howard Marks was being led off for processing, the other detective stopped him. In a tone of voice approaching awe, he asked, "Any more at home like you?"

It was now 11:00 A.M. The captain came in and put Hillary Marks' name on the board in green chalk. Mace called the lab and asked to be put through to Ballistics. Carol Zapata got on the line first.

"I'm headed out to the coroner's office," she said. "There's an autopsy scheduled at one o'clock. I think it's something you'll want to see." She paused before she added, "In the aquarium."

The aquarium was the glass-enclosed autopsy room where sensitive examinations were performed. Observers could watch the forensic doctors work from behind thick glass walls. If they wanted to hear what was being said, they had to wait and listen to the recording the doctors made while performing the autopsy. If Carol had been invited, that meant it involved a case she had special knowledge of. Mace thanked her.

"Anytime," she said, and he let the invitation linger. At his request, she transferred him to Ballistics.

When the technician picked up the phone, Mace asked if they had had a chance yet to fire the gun he recovered on Friday. He had requested that they match the casing and bullets to his Mancini evidence. The momentum of his morning was shattered when the technician informed him that the physical evidence had all been appropriated by RHD, who took everything to their own lab.

"How am I supposed to run my investigation if they take my evidence?"

The technician suggested that Mace take that up with his captain; it was out of his hands.

"Great," Mace muttered as he slammed down the phone. "Just fucking great."

At 12:45, he arrived at the Los Angeles coroner's office; Carol Zapata pulled in beside him. When she saw Mace, she checked her face in the mirror and swept her hand over her hair.

Her eyes were bright when she caught up to him. "I think the Butcher left us a whole corpse this time."

"C'mon." He grabbed Carol's arm. "I want to get a good seat."

They identified themselves in the anteroom and signed in. Before crossing through the locked doors, they pulled on warmer clothes. Mace had a wool-lined windbreaker and Carol a heavy turtleneck, which she put on under her lab coat. They passed through the larger autopsy room first. Bodies on steel carts lined the walls, awaiting dissection. Carol had to shout to be heard over the sound of the power saws and drills. Her breath fogged as she spoke.

"The rotation shift called me. The decedent was discovered early this morning by some fisherman. They called me because she's got similar ligature marks to the Glassen corpse."

"Does Ernie know about this?"

"Speak of the devil." Carol gestured over Mace's shoulder. He didn't have to turn around to know who had just arrived.

"I can't seem to shake the guy."

"It must be your magnetic personality," she said. "I didn't call him."

"Have they ID'd the stiff yet?"

"They ran her prints. She was a hooker in Venice. I'll get a copy of her sheet for you."

They pushed through the crowded autopsy arena. Microphones hung over eight gurneys filled with corpses in various stages of evisceration. He passed what had been a middle-aged woman. Her scalp had been slit across the top and the skin was pulled over her face like the peelings of some macabre fruit. There was a smell of fresh death in the air. As always, Mace was reminded of the summer spent on his uncle's farm, where he had helped his uncle gut a hog. It had been warm; the smell of raw bloody meat and intestines still loaded with undigested food had clung to his clothes for the entire day. His aunt had been disappointed when he only pushed his chops around his plate.

"You'll never be a farmer, boy," she had said. His uncle told her to leave him alone. It was his first time; he'd get used to it, the man had said.

He never had.

That smell returned to him now as he passed the body of a black male, his torso laid open with an inverted Y cut.

Carol left him to join the doctors inside the aquarium. From his vantage point, he studied the corpse. It was a young Caucasian woman, now gray with death. She lay naked on the examining table. The professionals gathered about her ignored the horror of her remains and turned to their work with a clinical eye. Carol pointed to the young woman's wrists and ankles and pointedly caught his eye. He nodded; the bruises there appeared to have been caused by chains. He watched Carol take exact measurements with her calipers. Another doctor swabbed the woman's vagina and anus. Both orifices showed signs of recent violent penetration. The flesh was torn. The entire abdominal cavity had also been shredded. The torso was stabbed so repeatedly that additional incisions were not needed to remove her organs, which Mace knew would be weighed and evaluated.

For Mace's benefit, Carol pointed to dried blood on the woman's inner thigh.

His mind's eye snapped a mental photograph. The blood was spread there in a deliberate fashion. A wavy pattern, three inches wide, extended from crotch to knee.

The door opened behind him and a familiar voice echoed off the walls. "What the fuck do you think you're doing?" Ernie Potts asked.

"I'm investigating a murder," Mace said without looking up. "But now I'm thinking it was probably a suicide."

Potts watched the autopsy for a few seconds; a slow smile spread over his face.

"I love it when the assholes kill one another," he said.

Mace twitched. They looked at each other in the reflection of the thick glass.

"You know what the trouble with you is, St. John?"

"What's that, Ernie?"

"You think this hamburger"—he nodded down below—"matters."

"Go to hell."

"You don't belong here. This is my investigation," Ernie barked. The veins pulsed on the top of his bald head. His bow tie was askew.

Mace consulted a paper in his hand. "Wait a minute, wrong corpse. I'm looking for a Hillary Marks."

Potts studied him with wary, hooded eyes.

"My mistake," Mace said. He allowed his shoulder to make solid contact with Ernie's chest as he pushed pass, and he was gratified when he heard Ernie's breath escape in a grunt.

After he left the basement, he took the elevator upstairs to the

162

Records Department, where his friend Mando worked. He found pandemonium. Stacks of handwritten reports, bulging manila file folders, and bundles of field identification cards held together with rubber bands spilled out of metal carts. Men sat on the floors, their ties loosened and shirtsleeves rolled up. The windowless room was thick with cigarette smoke and stale sweat. Mace reached toward the electric fan on a nearby desk and twelve officers raised their heads in horror and shouted, "No!" in unison.

Mace pulled his hand away slowly, palm up. "Don't shoot," he said.

"Man, don't scare us like that," the man sitting closest to the door said. "You almost set us back ten years."

The city had opened their coffers with the election of the new mayor. The new administration promised to be police-friendly, and the first gesture was the purchase of new electronic equipment to replace the city's outdated filing system. A lot of overtime was being clocked in the laborious processes of switching to automation. At poker on Friday night, Mando had groaned about the enormous task that lay ahead of them. All the data of the last fifty years had to be entered manually before the speed of automation could be enjoyed.

Mace noticed a new banner on the wall over the watercooler. It was printed on computer paper in big block dot matrix letters. He stopped and read the words. WHEN I DIE, I WANT TO GO LIKE MY GRANDFATHER, QUIETLY IN HIS SLEEP." The line below read NOT SCREAMING IN TERROR LIKE THE PASSENGER BESIDE HIM.

He chuckled and sought out his buddy's cubicle.

"Oh, man, they're killing me here," Mando said from behind a box of files. "I haven't seen my old lady in a week, with all this overtime."

"Well, at least someone's benefiting from all this." He picked up a framed picture sitting on the desk and admired the domestic bliss depicted there. Mando's wife, new baby, and golden retriever all grinned back at him. They all looked happy enough;

still, you never knew who was just hanging on by their fingernails. "I need a favor. Can you pull the record of Caroline Rhinehart for me?"

"Spell that last name. What's she done?"

"It would be a juvenile record. Probably about ten years old."

Mando switched on the screen at his desk. "Then it should be in the system." He was talking about CLETS, the California law-enforcement Teletype system.

"It would help if you knew the city where the arrests occurred."

"Santa Monica."

"Now I know why that name is familiar. Isn't she a probation officer?"

"It's personal."

He waited while Mando typed her name into the CLETS and pushed the search button.

"These new computers are supposed to make this job faster, but I don't trust them. Takes just as long to look up how to type in a request as it would to pull the hard copy manually. Wait a minute. Well, I'll be damned."

"What you got?" Mace asked.

"I don't believe it," Mando said.

"What? Is she an ax murderer or something?" Mace went around the desk so he could see the screen for himself.

"No, I don't believe it worked. I just put the name in and I got an answer."

"Well?"

"She's got a CII number." He was talking about the Criminal Information Index number assigned to anyone ever arrested. The computer beeped. A new line of information printed across the screen. "Wait a minute—I'm getting something else." He studied the coded information and pulled out his manual. After a moment, he looked up triumphantly, his finger marking a table of numbers and letters. "It couldn't have been anything too bad, according to the code. If she had a felony, she'd have a four-series number. Sex offenders are three-series. Ax murderers, that would be your five-series. Relax, bro, she's strictly minor league. Her number is a one-series."

"And?"

"Her record is sealed."

"Christ, Mando. I could have told you that much. Can't you find out anything more?"

"You need a court order for that. Unless . . ." Mando scooted his chair over to a clear section of his desk.

"Unless?"

"If you know when the arrest occurred, the department would have a record of the original investigation on hard copy. You'd still need a court order to see the final judicature, but not for the police reports."

"That would work."

"Santa Monica maintains its own records. I've got a buddy over there." Mando scribbled a name on a piece of paper and handed it to Mace. "I don't know his extension. Go see him; he'll help you out."

"Thanks, man. I owe you."

"You must like this girl. Last woman you ran through on a personal was your wife."

2∅

_____

When Mace returned to the station, he made several calls. The first was to Dr. Miller. His receptionist informed the detective that _Doctor_ was with a patient and would call at his earliest convenience.

Fifteen minutes later, Dr. Hymie Miller called. Mace recounted the details of the new victim's wounds and the curious smear pattern of blood on her inner thigh. The doctor asked for a minute to consider the ramifications of this new information.

At last he spoke. "Your offender is getting bolder. He no longer feels the need to go to such lengths to conceal his crime. He probably feels that if he's gotten away with it once, he will do so again. Quite possibly, he has been questioned already by your investigators. I see the stab wounds to the woman's abdomen as further proof of the killer's need to penetrate his victim in a painful manner. You are assuming that the women were nude at the time of death, correct?"

"That's right," Mace said. "We found no fibers on the bullet and none by the cuts. The weapons would have carried fabric with them into the body."

"This strengthens the validity our first theories of a sexual sadist."

"What do you make of the blood smears?" Mace asked. "I'm

certain they were made intentionally and not the result of random action."

"Yes, I've given that some thought. It sounds almost ritualistic. I believe it was a symbolic gesture on the part of the murderer. His blood lust satisfied, he makes a loving gesture. In his own twisted way, perhaps he is thanking the woman. It won't stop here. Your man will kill again. The thirst for blood, if you'll pardon my melodrama, is like an addiction—an addiction with a steadily rising level of tolerance. He will kill again and he will do it soon."

Mace thanked the doctor for his help and hung up. He drummed his fingers on the desk for a minute; then he grabbed the phone book and looked up the number of the free clinic on Brooks Avenue. Mondays were Nan's do-it-for-free day.

"What's wrong?" she asked when she came to the phone. "Is it Digger?"

"I need your help."

"With what?"

"You've heard about the Ballona Creek Butcher?"

"Sure. How can I help with that?"

"The first victim, Victoria Glassen, had venereal disease. I need to know if she was treated for it and if she filled out a list of sexual partners."

"You know that's confidential information. I can't . . . Did you say the *first* victim? Has there been another?"

"They just found her. According to your boyfriend, it won't be stopping with two; actually, the death toll is three—that we know of."

"The records are kept at the downtown office. I'm going in tomorrow. I'll check it out and call you if I come up with something."

"Thanks, Nan."

"Anytime," she said softly.

He hung up the phone and wondered what Freud would have made of that answer.

*　*　*

MUNCH spent most of Monday tearing apart the top of the engine of the Dodge. She was glad to be busy. The temptation was strong just to leave now. Her car was running; she had new identification and a little bit of money. Of course, now that she had begun the valve job on the Dodge, she felt obligated to see it through. It wouldn't be right to leave the pieces for someone else to put back together. No, Ruby was right: She had to stop running sometime.

She climbed inside the engine compartment of the Dodge to make a final check that she was ready to proceed to the last stage of the teardown. She ran her hand along the back of the engine to make sure nothing was still attached. A forgotten wire or hose could cause a big problem when it came time to start yanking.

Finally, she was satisfied that all the bolts that held the cylinder heads to the block were out and all the other accessories safely out of the way. She'd seen other mechanics get into big trouble at this point, break expensive parts because they didn't take that extra minute to make sure they were all clear. This was where, she always thought, being strong could work against you. Better to be smart and have to think the job through, rather than to be a bull who tore things apart indiscriminately and made the reassembly part that more difficult. From now on, she was going to apply those principles to her personal life as well, if she was given the chance. First things first, she reminded herself.

Using a big pry bar that she wedged into an exhaust port, she pried the head apart from the block. The remaining coolant and oil bled together, green and black, down the side of the engine. Her hands were slippery with the oily fluids. She wiped them on a rag and considered her next move. Jack had specifically told her not to try to lift the heads herself. This asking for help all the time was a constant lesson in humility. That was supposed to be a good thing. Somehow, it was supposed to be a way to get closer to God, more in touch with her own feelings. If she got any closer to her feelings, they would have to put her in the nuthouse. She always seemed to be on the verge of tears. Ruby said to hang on, that it would get better. She even gave her a bumper sticker that read DON'T GIVE UP FIVE MINUTES BEFORE THE MIRACLE.

They had a lot of little sayings at the meetings: "Easy does it"; "One day at a time"; "First things first"; and, her personal favorite, "Today I live."

First things first, she reminded herself again. That meant getting these seventy-pound heads to the ground. Lou walked by and she called to him. "Can you help me?"

"Heavy, aren't they?" he said.

She waited for him to make some crack. He surprised her by helping her lift the heads to the ground without so much as a snicker. She jumped down from the car and turned the heads upside down so that she could study them. The intake valve that was stuck open had black crystals fused to its beveled edges and was heat-warped.

She and Lou exchanged looks.

"We better flush the gas tank on this one," Lou said.

"Have you met this guy?" she asked.

"Yeah, he's an asshole. Mr. Disco. I think he's going through a divorce."

"That kind always is," she said.

She used the phone in the office to call the machine shop. They said they would be there within the hour to pick up the heads. After she hung up with them, she pulled a business card out of her pocket and dialed the number printed in black. She got goose bumps when she read the guy's name. Ruby said that when that happened, it was because there was an angel tapping you on the shoulder.

"SARGE?" Cassiletti said to him when he returned to the squad room. "You got a call on line two, some girl."

"Sergeant St. John, Homicide," he said as he picked up the call.

"I was close, wasn't I?"

His heart skipped a beat. "What do I call you now?"

"Munch will do. I have something you want."

"If you're talking about the gun, I already have it."

He heard a sharp intake of breath. "What about our deal?" she asked.

"What else do you have that I want?" he asked her.

Another intake of breath.

Munch had spent the weekend debating that very question. She didn't want to be a snitch. She had been raised to believe that a snitch was the lowest form of life. Ruby insisted that this was "stinking thinking," as she put it. Munch would have to change her value system, Ruby insisted. That sort of thinking had gotten her where she was. But Munch knew there was more to it than that. If she told the detective where she got the gun, she would be incriminating herself. Ruby reminded her that she had turned her will and life over to the care of her Higher Power; this was no time to be taking it back.

Munch countered with the loophole she had found in the step about making amends. It says, she pointed out to her sponsor, that you should make amends only when to do so would not injure *yourself* or others. Ruby hadn't known how to respond to that other than to say, "Turn it over."

"If I tell you where I got the gun," she asked him now, "will you square things for me?"

"I'll do my best."

"Why should I trust you?"

"You called me."

"Let me go over this with you and I'll tell you the parts I'm having trouble with."

"Lay it on me."

"That's what he said."

"What?"

"Sorry, bad joke." She giggled, sounding like a little girl. "Okay, seriously. Say a person is suspected of a criminal act with a weapon and the police take a statement from that person about how they came into possession of that weapon. Wouldn't that person be incredibly stupid to implicate themselves?"

"Who have you been talking to?" Mace asked. If she had a lawyer, that would change things.

"I'm just trying to get clear on this," she said.

"I'm going to level with you. If a certain weapon was used in the commission of a crime, several crimes, and the first crime it was used for was of more importance to the police than the second crime, then in that scenario, a deal could be agreed on."

"Hypothetically speaking, couldn't the information the police sought be obtained over the phone?"

He snorted impatiently. "If you want my help," he said, discarding the pretense, "You'll have to make your statements in person, so I have proper documentation. To make anything stick, I have to have a solid chain of evidence. How about if I meet you somewhere?"

"I was hoping to keep this off the record."

"I can't promise that."

"This has to do with the Ballona Creek Butcher murder, doesn't it?"

"What makes you say that?" He sat up suddenly. Cassiletti raised an eyebrow and reached for the extension. Mace waved him away.

"I read the paper, the way that girl died. It must have been horrible. It could have been me."

"He's struck again, a hooker named . . ." He scrambled for the sheet of the latest victim. "Brenda Wallace." A sudden instinct told him to share this with the girl. The sharp intake of breath on the other end of the line informed him that his gut feeling had been right on. "He won't stop. I need your help."

A moment of silence and then she said, "I'll meet you tomorrow night. Do you know where Lairs is?"

"On Washington and Lincoln?"

"Yeah."

"Why not tonight?" he asked.

"I have a prior commitment," she said.

"All right. What time tomorrow?"

"Seven." Then she said something that struck him as odd. "Maybe we can save each other."

Mace hung up the phone and wondered what she'd meant by that.

21

The restaurant that Mace usually took his dad to on Monday nights for ribs was decorated in a Polynesian motif. Tapa paper covered the walls, and the ceilings were lined with dry palm fronds, curled with age. Tiki lanterns lit the bar, where long-haired women in bikini tops and grass skirts circulated with fragrant leis that hung in woven baskets on leather thongs around their necks. Similarly clad woman served drinks in coconut shells with little umbrellas stuck in them.

They took their customary table near the patio. A waterfall cascaded over red-brown lava rocks and fake parrots perched in miniature palms. The sound of the water was soothing. But his selection of tables went beyond the meager aural pleasures the fountain provided. As usual, Mace's reasons for always choosing that table were two-fold. If the place ever caught on fire, he wanted to be near open air. Without asking, the waitress brought Mace a Seven-and-Seven in a bucket glass and a ginger ale for Digger.

"Thanks, Shirley," he said.

She brushed against him and asked if he wanted anything else. He smiled and asked her to bring them dinner when it was convenient.

After she was gone, Digger grunted. "She wants you."

"Yeah, yeah," Mace said, "you always say that."

"They always do."

To change the subject, Mace told his dad about his ongoing investigation.

"You still working on that chicken thing?"

Digger was having one of his good days. When Mace arrived at the house, his father had been dressed and ready in clothes that almost matched. That he remembered an event as recent as a month ago was another promising sign.

"He hit again. This time, he left the whole body. It's the same guy; I can feel it."

Digger sipped his drink and made a face. "They forgot to put the booze in this again."

"I'll tell them about it, Dad."

"You know, your case reminds me about something that was in the news."

"Same case—they just published the details."

"Terrible thing to do to a dog."

"What dog? What are you talking about, Dad?"

"That kid that tore the legs off the dogs. Don't you remember?"

Mace looked at his dad in exasperation. His dad's recollections were all jumbled up. He'd often juxtapose people and places in his stories, and Mace knew they couldn't have been where he said they were, when they were. Then he'd remember something with surprising accuracy that had happened thirty years ago. "When was this?"

"Years ago, when my son was in the service."

"I'm your son, Dad."

Digger stared at him hard, his face working as he struggled to assimilate his thoughts. "That's right. You were in the service. The cops caught some kid in the Ballona wetlands. He had a whole torture chamber set up in some abandoned house or something. He was chaining up stray dogs and pulling them apart while they were still alive. They caught him, though. Sick son of a bitch."

"Sounds like it."

Shirley brought their salad and asked if everything was all right.

Digger winked pointedly at his son. Mace sighed.

"I think we're close to catching this guy, too."

"Good," Digger said. "You were always good at catching the guy, weren't you?"

"I still am."

The ribs arrived and the conversation ceased as both men got busy devouring their dinner.

22

At the Monday-night meeting of Narcotics Anonymous, held at a clubhouse in North Hollywood named, aptly enough, the Survivors Club, Munch led her first meeting. She was now nine days clean and sober. The format of the meeting was discussion, followed by a twenty-minute speech.

They were seated in folding metal chairs arranged around a large rectangular table. After reading the preamble, Munch began the sharing.

"My name is Daisy," she said, "and I'm an addict and an alcoholic."

The others around the table responded by saying, "Hi, Daisy."

"I found out today that someone I used to run with died. Brenda was like a sister to me. We went through a lot together. She was the one who taught me how to put on makeup—how to heat up the eyeliner pencil and line the bottom of my lower lid on the inside of my lashes. I know that might not sound like much, but I never had a mom to show me stuff like that."

This news was greeted with knowing nods and murmurs of "I heard that" and "That's cold."

"Brenda was always there for me," Munch continued. "The last time I saw her was right before I got clean and sober."

They had gone flat-backing together. A black guy who called himself Commander took them around to the projects where the wetbacks lived twelve to a room. He always brought at least two girls on the runs because the Mexicans had some sort of code against screwing the same woman as their brother. Commander charged ten dollars a pop—the object was volume. He gave the girls seven of the ten dollars. That night, she had made $154, Brenda even more. Tears rolled down Munch's cheeks as she remembered the telephone conversation she had had with her friend. Brenda called the next morning and said she had gone home, sat in the bathtub, and just cried.

"I wish I could tell her that she didn't have to live that way." She wiped the tears stinging her eyes. "I've never been clean this long before." Munch shook her head in disbelief. "I have a confession to make." She looked around the room. "My name isn't really Daisy; it's Munch."

The people around the table greeted this news with laughter. "Keep coming back," someone called out.

"Who's next?" she asked, and called on a man who raised his hand.

At the coffee break, Ruby gave her a hug. "I'm sorry about your friend. Just say to yourself, 'There but for the grace of God go I.'"

"Yeah," she answered, "well, sometimes God needs a little help."

Ruby looked at her knowingly. "Sometimes, it seems that way."

After the meeting, a man approached Munch. "We're going for coffee," he said. "Would you like to join us?" He was attractive—dark curly hair and matching mustache, clear brown eyes. He smiled when he spoke to her, revealing even white teeth. He said his name was Don H.

"I . . . can't," she said. "I've . . . got my period."

"It's just coffee," he said. "There'll be a bunch of us, men and women."

She blushed when she realized her assumption.

"It's okay," the guy said. "Just keep coming back. It gets better."

ON Tuesday morning, Nan called Mace.

"I made a copy of Vicky Glassen's file," she told him. "I think I have something you can use."

"Great."

He heard a rustle of papers; then Nan spoke again. "Her case was earmarked. The strain of gonorrhea that she had is a new one and still rare. We're calling it PPNG. It has penicillinase properties, which means that we can't treat it the same way we normally treat gonorrhea, because the bacterial enzymes in the virus inactivates penicillin."

"What do you use?"

"Spectinomycin seems to be effective."

"Can you put together the list of people who have been infected for me?" he asked.

"It'll take some time. When do you need it?"

"Yesterday."

"I'll get going on it. Give me your telex number."

He read it off to her.

"Dr. Miller wants to talk to you. He's thought of a few more things. He'll call you later."

"I'll be in court most of the day; tell him to leave a message with Dispatch."

The last call he made was to Jimbo Washington, his colleague in Vice.

"Do you have a file of freaks?" A freak was a john who beat up prostitutes.

"Any kind in particular?" Jimbo asked.

"I'm looking for a guy who chains the girls up. Anything like that?"

"I'll check it out. What's up?"

"We got a homicide involving a hooker victim."

"Anyone I know?" Jimbo asked.

"Brenda Wallace?"

"Shit."

"You knew her?"

"A lot of us knew her. How did she get it?"

"She was tortured and stabbed. That's why I'm calling."

"There is one guy the girls have been complaining about. I don't have a name."

"Let's get an artist to make a composite."

"I'm on it, bunkie."

LATER that morning, as he sat in the back of a Santa Monica courtroom and waited for his turn to testify, the conversation with Digger kept echoing in his head. He put it together with the information the psychiatrist, Dr. Miller, had supplied him with. Whoever this guy was, he must have left a shadow. What if he was a local? His sickness hadn't come out of nowhere. Somewhere this guy had a past, other records of sadistic behavior. Caroline had agreed to have lunch with him at the recess. He had planned for them to go to Bob Burns for an intimate lunch in the dark restaurant; now he didn't want to waste time. He wondered if she'd mind if instead they got sandwiches to go from the cafeteria.

The lawyers went into sidebar discussion with the judge and Mace stepped out into the hallway to call headquarters and check on his messages.

Cassiletti answered and told him that a list of names had arrived on the Teletype from his ex-wife. Mace told him that he'd pick them up after court.

"I've got a meeting with the shooter in the Mancini homicide at seven tonight at the Lairs," he told him.

"Are we bringing her in?" Cassiletti asked.

"Let's see what we get from her. She wants to cut a deal. In fact, I think it would be better if I go by myself. I don't want to spook her."

"Does she have a lawyer?"

"I doubt it; she didn't mention anything about a lawyer. If I know this broad, she'll come alone. She doesn't have anyone."

After he hung up with Mace, Cassiletti placed another call. "I've got an update for you," he said.

23

Court broke for an hour's lunch recess and Mace found Caroline waiting for him in the hallway.

"I need to check something out at the animal shelter," he said to her. "Would you mind a lunch on the run?"

While they bought ready-made sandwiches, she asked, "Why do you need to go there?"

"My dad mentioned something at dinner last night—something he remembered from about ten, maybe fifteen years ago about a kid who tortured animals."

"Isn't your dad sort of . . ."

"What?"

"Never mind. What were you saying?"

"I'd like to stop over at the SPCA, see if anyone there remembers the incident."

"Does this have to do with a murder investigation?"

"It might tie in to the Glassen case. This shrink I talked to said that the offender probably had an earlier history of sadistic behavior. That makes sense to me."

"Once a criminal, always a criminal?" she asked. She posed the question quietly.

He hesitated before he answered; instinct warned him that he had just entered a minefield—something in her tone of voice, the arch of her eyebrows.

"I'm not talking about joyriding," he said, then realized too late he had detonated a booby trap.

"Joyriding?" she asked. "What an interesting choice of juvenile offenses to choose from. Why did that come to mind?"

They had reached the parking lot. He slipped his key in the door of the car and avoided her eyes. "Do you want to go or not?" he asked.

"Oh, I'd love to see you in action, Detective. So much goes on behind the scenes, don't you think? Where we civilians don't have a clue." She got in the passenger seat and folded her hands primly on her lap.

As he walked around to the driver's side, he stole a glance skyward. "Here we go, folks," he said out loud. Sometimes, he had an incredibly big mouth.

THE westside chapter of the Society for Prevention of Cruelty to Animals was sandwiched between warehouses on a cul-de-sac in the industrial section of Santa Monica—a collection of storage buildings and body shops near the bus station. Shopping carts full of derelicts' wordly goods parked in doorways served as declarations of homesteading claims. Blanket rolls, layers of newspaper, and empty wine bottles spilled onto the sidewalk. Mace couldn't help but wonder about a civilization that sheltered and fed its stray animals and left the humans to face the elements alone. Of course, the hospitality extended to the animals lasted only so long. No easy answers. He snuck a look at Caroline's angry face. None at all.

They parked the car near the entrance of the pound and were greeted by the prolonged barking (judging by the variety of pitch and volume) of every conceivable size of dog. They were welcomed at the front desk by a round-faced gentleman in his sixties who smiled as they entered. He transferred the leash he was holding to his left hand and extended his right to Mace. Then he came around from behind the desk with his charge in tow.

"How can I help you?" he asked, beaming broadly, as if welcoming rich customers to a Beverly Hill's showroom. He reached down and stroked the neck of the black-and-white Labrador mix tethered beneath him. The dog responded by lovingly licking his face.

Mace handed the man a business card. "I wonder if you can answer a few questions for me."

"About a homicide?" The man looked nervously between the two of them. "Caroline Rhinehart?" he asked, noticing her for the first time.

"Hello, Angel," she said. "Detective St. John is investigating an incident that happened a long time ago, to dogs."

Mace looked between the two of them in surprise. He decided to let Caroline tell him in her own time how the two of them knew each other.

"Certainly, Detective, anything I can do," Angel said.

"Do you remember an incident—I'm going back ten, fifteen years—where dogs were dismembered?"

"It was before I started working here," he said, and winked at Caroline. "But something like that gets talked about. Nothing outrages folks more than cruelty to animals. Johnson was bombing the shit out of North Vietnam, but the dog dismemberment made the front page of the *L.A. Times.*"

"What else do you remember?"

"Just that some teenager was torturing dogs. He pulled off their legs while they were still alive. Happened over in the Ballona wetlands, but they brought the animals here. Neighbors heard the animals crying and turned him in. That put an end to that. The kid was just under eighteen, so his name wasn't published. If you want any more details, you might want to come back tomorrow. Talk to Ed. He was working here back then. He's off Tuesdays, but he'll be here in the morning." The animal on the leash gave a drawn-out whimper and nudged Angel's legs. Angel crooned to the animal, "Don't worry, you'll get your bone." The dog licked his hands and lowered the front of her body till her head rested on her outstretched paws. Her butt stayed in the air. She gave off one sharp yap and wagged her tail. Then she jumped to her feet again.

Mace reached down and patted the animal's head. The dog responded by wagging her tail and dropping open her mouth in what could only be interpreted as a grin. It was then that he noticed the animal's startling blue eyes, so light that they were almost white.

"Great eyes," he said. She obviously knew how to use them to her advantage, batting them now coyly. When Mace smiled at her and made a little kissing sound, she cocked her head sidewise and her ears perked up in an imitation of the RCA Victor logo dog.

"Yeah, we think she must have some husky in her," Angel said.

"You give the dogs bones?" Mace asked. "Nice life."

"Just the ones on death row, sort of a last meal treat." Angel scratched the dog behind her ears and her tail thumped the counter.

"Death row?" Mace asked, and stole a look at the happy animal.

"Yeah, she's been with us for three weeks. Her time has come. She's real smart, make a great companion."

"A good watchdog, too, I imagine," Caroline said.

As if on cue, the dog jumped up on Mace, planting two white paws on his chest and licking his face. He was aware of Caroline watching him.

"Maybe I'll adopt her," he said. "My dad could use a watchdog."

"I'll start the paperwork," Angel said. "Her name is Samantha."

Ten minutes later, they were headed for the exit: Caroline, Mace, and a reluctant Samantha, who dug her paws in the linoleum as they approached the front door. "What's with her?" Mace asked.

"She doesn't want to leave Nicky."

"Who's Nicky?"

"Her cagemate," Angel said. "I've never seen two female animals take to each other more. They sleep with their heads on each other's stomachs, play together, groom each other. Ah, well, she'll get over it." He opened up the cage under his desk and extracted an English sheepdog mix with big brown eyes. "C'mon, Nicky," Angel said. "I've got a nice bone for you, sweetheart."

IN the car, on the way to Digger's, Caroline asked, "How's your dad going to like having two new dogs?"

Mace shrugged. "You heard the man—you can't split up a pair like that. Maybe I'll keep them with me for a while and make sure that they're going to work out."

"Don't you want to run a make on them?" She reached around to the backseat and petted the dogs, which were busy slobbering up the rear windows and equally oblivious to each other.

He looked skyward again. "All right, I'm sorry. I didn't mean to invade your privacy. How did you find out?"

"The guy in Records, the one you asked to violate the court order?"

"Wait a minute," he said. "Technically, I didn't unseal any records. I just asked him to look up the original arrest reports. But anyhow, what about him?"

"He's my cousin."

"Oh. Small world, huh?"

She nodded.

He decided to risk another question. "By the way, where did you know the guy at the shelter from?"

"Angel? I got him his job." A smile played on her lips. "Actually, it started as community service."

"The guy was a client of yours?"

"Does this relate to your investigation, or is this a personal?"

He sighed. "Mea culpa."

She cracked open her window and let her purse rest on the seat between them, instead of clutching it in her lap. He took this as a sign of encouragement. "Just one question—what was Angel on probation for?"

"He's a con artist." She looked at him. "Was."

Mace stole a glance in the rearview mirror and Samantha panted back at him. Her big red tongue lolled to the side of her mouth, saliva dropping to the seat, and her eyes closed in a squint, till only a slit of blue showed through. It was an expression that could easily be interpreted as laughter. Nicky batted her big brown eyes in sort of an apology and then threw up on the floor.

As they turned onto the boulevard, Mace checked his watch. "Do you mind if we make a quick stop?" He made a right turn. "My place is about six blocks from here, on Olympic. I can't leave the dogs in the car." As if to emphasize his point, Samantha began chewing on the armrest. "Hey, stop that!" he yelled at her. She barked and began cleaning the inside of his ear.

"You're really good with dogs," Caroline said, and quickly looked out the window.

Five minutes later, they arrived at the Bella Donna.

When he opened the car door, the two dogs tumbled out, barking joyfully. They chased each other around the train, playing tag by biting each other on the scruff of the neck. Then after somersaults and pretend snarls, they changed directions and the new "it" dog became the chaser.

"Does your heart good, doesn't it?" Caroline said.

Mace realized he was grinning. He wondered how long it had been since the animals had had a good run.

Tired of their game, the animals reconnoitered. Mace watched as they paced off the perimeter, noses to the ground. The two dogs stopped at intervals to squat and mark their territory. After a few minutes, they returned to stand at their human savior's side.

He ruffled their ears. "Thirsty?"

They panted yes.

He opened the gate of the platform and swung the intricately ornate wrought-iron outward. Then he lifted up the steel plate that interrupted the stairway and led his charges up the stairs. As he opened his door, it occurred to him that this was the first time he had let someone in in a long, long time.

Nicky and Sam bounded up the stairs gracefully, as if they had always belonged there. Caroline followed. He felt himself holding his breath.

"Oh," she said as she entered his parlor. "It's wonderful."

The first thing she did was cross the floor and sit down at the piano. She ran her hands over the ivory keys. He had never seen anything so desirable in his life as those delicate fingers resting on the keys.

"Play something," he said.

She turned to him. Her eyes were smoky and unreadable. Her face froze and her lips parted, as if she was going to say something. He'd seen the look many times; it usually preceded a confession. The moment felt suddenly intense, as though there was too much feeling packed into one tiny space. Whatever she had to say, he knew that it would mark a new level of intimacy between them. This time, he didn't look away.

"He didn't show you my entire arrest history."

"It doesn't matter."

"It might."

"It won't."

"I want to tell you." She stared directly into his eyes and began. "I told you I ran with a rough crowd. I ran away from home when I was fourteen. My father drank; my mother looked the other way. I met a man who said he loved me and I ran off with him. He turned out to be a junkie. He used me to run scams on people. Usually, I'd be the security he'd leave with people he was scoring drugs for."

"Little Miss Marker?" he asked, smiling gently to encourage her.

She looked at him levelly; he could see the effort to tell him was taking a lot of courage. Seated on the little piano bench, she threw back her shoulders and continued. "It was my job to escape somehow before the people realized they'd been had. Sometimes I did, sometimes not." She took a deep breath and looked down. "Then I had to placate the people anyway I could. I did what I had to."

"We all do." He went to her and took her hand. "But you're okay now; you did good. You turned your life around."

"I had help. No matter how far down I got, how low I sunk, I could always hear, even when I seemed unreachable. I remember every kind word ever spoken to me, every hand that ever reached out."

He heard a siren in the distance. Duty called. He glanced at the clock above the bar. "I've got to get back to court." He was still holding her hand, unwilling to let the moment pass. "I've done things, too—things I'm not proud of." He stopped there.

She waited but didn't ask.

"After work, let's get together. You can come over to my dad's house with me and help me explain to him about the dogs."

She smiled. "I'd like that."

"I have something to do at seven." He gave her a set of keys. "Would you mind meeting me here? We'll need some dog food, too. Would you mind . . ."

She held up her hands in surrender. "Okay, Detective. I'll be here. I'll feed the dogs. I'll wait for you. But—"

"But?"

"I don't want you to hold back on me." She stood up and they stood eye-to-eye. "I expect one hundred percent. That's the way it has to be."

"That's what I want, too." As he said the words, they surprised him, but he knew they were true.

24

At six o'clock on Tuesday, Munch was ready to go. The trip to Venice would take thirty to forty-five minutes, but she couldn't see the point in hanging around the motel any longer. She had dressed quickly, too nervous to bother with makeup. She selected a pair of white bell-bottoms and a red-and-white-striped top. On her way out the door, she grabbed her coat.

As she got on the freeway, she fingered the amulet Ruby had given her. It was a pewter medal of St. Jude on a thin silver chain. Only when pressed did Ruby admit that St. Jude was the patron saint of hopeless causes and desperate situations.

The sign above the restaurant was soon visible when she got off the freeway, a large yellow lion with his mouth open in a roar. Lairs seemed an appropriate meeting place. She, the proverbial Christian, off to meet the lion in his den. Maybe that wasn't quite the parallel she wanted. Didn't the lions usually win?

She was early. The waitress asked her how many in her party.

"Two," Munch said, "Maybe three. I'll just wait for them by the door here."

She was standing by the horoscope machine near the cash register when she heard the familiar rumble. Instinctively, she turned to the sounds. A second later, she spotted the bikes roaring down Lincoln. She counted close to twenty of them through the plate-glass window that fronted the Lairs, all solo riders. She panicked when she realized that the lead bike, a black Sportster, was driven by Crazy Mike. He was followed by what appeared to be the entire club. At the flower shop next to the restaurant, they peeled off in to two groups.

Oh God, she thought, they're coming here.

If she ran out the door to Lincoln Boulevard, where her car was parked, she wouldn't get far. It was too open, too exposed. Her only hope was to reach the back parking lot before they did; then maybe she could elude them on foot. She darted toward the back of the restaurant, past the startled waitress, and knocked down a busboy with a load of dirty dishes. The resulting confusion of broken pottery and his huddled form as he attempted to clean the mess up barred her exit through the kitchen. She made a quick pivot and headed toward the cocktail lounge. On her way to the swinging doors of the bar, she grabbed at the place settings for some kind of weapon and dumped what she could in her pocket. The lounge had its own separate door, which exited to the parking lot on Washington. She burst through to the outside and was blinded by headlights. The second group of bikers had reached the parking lot before her.

"Get on." Crazy Mike gestured to the back of his bike. "No bullshit this time."

MACE was westbound on Washington. He looked over in time to witness the abduction. It was obvious the girl wasn't willing. Her head whipped around wildly, like an animal caught in a snare. He was trapped in traffic. Even if he could get to her, what chance would he have against the pack of twenty bikers? He had to try. He put his car in park and vaulted the center divider guardrail. Cars heading east refused to slow down. She spotted him and pleaded with her eyes for him to help. Beyond her, he recognized Ugly Bud, the DEA agent. The bikes took off in unison, weaving their way through traffic.

Mace raced back to his car and got on the radio to call for backup. He paused in midsentence with the microphone in his hand. Something about the girl as she drove off on the back of the motorcycle. What was it that he recognized as so disturbingly familiar? It was the oil, the spray of black oil up the back of her white pants—the grease that had been thrown upward off the un-guarded drive chain of the Harley, leaving a pattern of drops up the back of her right leg. The oil on Vicky Glassen's leg had been in the same pattern. He threw down the microphone and pulled a quick illegal U-turn, bouncing off of parked cars, but it was al-ready too late. The motorcycles had maneuvered through the traf-fic and had disappeared.

THE Satan's Pride clubhouse and methamphetamine factory was a wooden structure that had served as a lounge for hunters, a place to clean the ducks they had bagged and to warm their bodies in the winter. It suited the bikers' needs well. The roar of airplanes taking off and landing masked the sound of the motorcycles. The building was nestled at the base of the Westchester bluffs and was accessible only by winding dirt paths. Smaller, low-lying duck blinds attached to the main house on either side formed a wide horseshoe. The adobe-walled duck blinds were where the bikers manufactured their drugs, always mindful of the fire hazard since the unfortunate razing of their last factory. The larger building was camouflaged by a giant cottonwood and the entire complex lay abandoned and forgotten. The Pride made use of what re-mained there. They erected their own pennants where the hunters' trophies had once stood. The walls were adorned with stolen freeway signs, souvenirs of places the Pride had visited. Other bike club colors hung upside down from the ceiling, their meaning clear. Several sagging couches with missing legs replaced by phone books and stuffing oozing out through ripped upholstery lined the walls. A black-and-white sign that read TURN OUT hung tilted so that it pointed to the clubhouse's upper level. The second floor was actually a loft, originally meant for storage, and accessible only by ladder. Mattresses lined the flooring in between the ceiling joists.

One of the Pride's members had worked for Pacific Gas and Electric and knew how to hook up a meter so that it didn't record the pirated usage of power.

On the ride to the clubhouse, billboards along Jefferson pleaded with people to save the terns and the titmice before the land became polluted beyond redemption. Carcasses of stolen and stripped modes of conveyance, everything from shopping carts to an overturned and rusting Ford Pinto, poked out from the bubbling stew of fecund water. Plastic by-products from a now-defunct limousine manufacturer gave rise to an unpleasant aroma of Bondo and resin. Even the salt grass and sea blight struggled to survive. Rising above the mire were black creosote-soaked telephone poles connected by power lines that buzzed like angry bees. The current hissed across the wetlands on its way to deliver power to posh Marina del Rey; a wire dipped occasionally to supply electricity to well meters. The only other sign of civilization was the pay phone by the side of the road. The location of the clubhouse was a closely guarded secret. The women who visited there had to submit to a blindfold first. No one had bothered to blindfold Munch. She read this as a bad sign.

The bikers parked their motorcycles in the courtyard. Crazy Mike produced two pairs of handcuffs, which he used to shackle her. He snapped one pair around her wrists and used the second pair to bind her ankle to the railing.

"Sorry, Bud," Crazy Mike said to a biker with a blue panhead, "the meeting's for members only. Stay out here and guard the bitch. We shouldn't be too long."

As soon as the bikers disappeared inside the clubhouse, Ugly Bud left at a jog for the street. She worked her hand out of the cuffs but could do nothing about the pair that held her ankle. She emptied the contents of the pockets of her coat.

Inside the clubhouse, she knew they were discussing her fate. The last thing she wanted was another trip to the upstairs loft.

She had been drunk and stoned the last time they took her there. Even then, it was a horrific experience as one biker after another took a turn with her. The worst of the lot had been Crazy Mike, urging his brothers on and watching it all. He came up the ladder when he learned that she was talking some of the more reluctant members of his club out of raping her.

"It's not rape," he had proclaimed. "This bitch has been paid for."

That's when she first learned of the deal Flower George had struck.

In her aborted flight from Lairs, she had cleared a table setting from a side booth and dumped what she could grab into the deep pockets of her coat. She felt for the set of flatware consisting of fork, knife, and spoon—any one of which might double as a weapon. She grabbed the knife in her right hand. She'd carve out eyes before she'd let them use her again. She stole a look at the clubhouse and at the road beyond where the other biker had disappeared. The motorcycles lay within reach. She'd hit them where it hurt. The assholes cared more about their bikes than their women. With every weapon in her arsenal, Munch attacked the Harleys. The guys would kill her when they discovered what she was doing. But at this point, she figured, they'd kill her anyway.

If she was lucky, in their rage, they would be quick about it. She knew all about the slow ways to die.

Once they had had her upstairs that time, they had kept after her for what seemed an eternity—certainly long after the effects of whatever intoxication she was under had worn off. They had kept drinking and snorting speed, all except Crazy Mike, who never took anything. This had made him all the more ominous. The others, as depraved as they were, at least had the excuse that they were operating under the influence of chemicals. Mike was just plain crazy, crazy and cruel. He had been the hardest to fool.

At some point of that awful night, she didn't know what time it was, she had lost all track of time; she just went limp. Some animal instinct had told her to feign sleep. When Crazy Mike shoved the steel tip of his motorcycle between her naked legs, she remained impassive. She willed her eyes closed and mouth slack. At length, he gave up and went back downstairs. That's when she overheard their final plans for her and she knew she had to escape.

The voices inside the clubhouse now reached a crescendo, led by their president. She read it as an announcement of the end of their halftime festivities before the conclusion of the big game— the game she didn't want to be in. Her hands shook as she labored over the motorcycles she could reach. Now she was certain that the meeting was breaking up. They were coming back outside to finish what they had started. Sounds of doors closing and boots clomping against the wooden floor of the clubhouse signaled their imminent arrival. Soon, the door would open and they would pour out, primed by wine and speed to do whatever their leader had convinced them they must do for the sake of the group.

The other biker returned first, the one they called Ugly Bud. She scooted back to the position where he had left her. She put her hands behind her back as if she was still bound by the cuffs, but now her hand clutched the serrated steak knife she had stolen from the restaurant.

He bent over her and she tensed herself to strike out at him, biding her time till he got closer.

Then he looked over and noticed the massacred motorcycles. Coils wires were severed, tires flattened, and ignition switches ripped out. Gas poured from open petcocks and fork marks waved through custom paint jobs. "Oh shit," he said as the rest of the pack approached.

25

Crazy Mike reached them first and took in the scene. "I told you to watch her," he said to Ugly Bud. Without looking at Munch, he sent her to the ground with a violent backhand slap. The heavy rings he wore cut through her cheek and broke open a two-inch gash along the bone. She fell back, unable to maintain her balance with her ankle manacled and hands behind her. He kicked her once in the side of her head and she was still.

Ugly Bud grabbed his arm and pulled him back before Crazy Mike could deliver a second kick. "I only left for a minute," he said. "I had to take a piss."

Crazy Mike pulled a gun from the pocket of his motorcycle jacket. "Did you get shy all of a sudden? Why didn't you just piss right here?"

"Shit, I don't know, man. Habit, I guess. Hey, I'm sorry about the bikes. I'll pay for them, okay?"

Mike approached with the gun, a large revolver. He cocked the pistol and brought it to Ugly Bud's temple. "Are you a cop, man?" he asked.

"What do you mean, am I cop?" Sweat trickled down his face. He forced a laugh. "What are you, nuts, man?"

Mike pulled the trigger and stepped back as the body crumpled to the ground, "Wrong answer, man."

Stinky pulled at Mike's sleeve. "We better get out of here, dude."

Crazy Mike swung around to the other bikers. "Everybody, double up." He wrapped the chain he used to lock up his bike around the dead DEA agent's ankles and then tied the other end to a loop welded to the back strut of his bike. He started his bike with one kick and put it in gear. "I'll dump the body and meet you guys in Topanga Canyon."

"What about her?" Stinky asked, pointing toward Munch.

"She'll ride with me," he said. "I've got special plans for her. Undo her ankle." He reached down and grabbed her by the back of her jacket. With one heave, he pulled her limp body across his lap.

Wary of the gun still clutched in Crazy Mike's hand, Stinky said, "I don't know about this. Maybe we should all lay low for a while."

"Yeah," another biker added, "it's too hot. I'm gonna split for a while."

Mike turned on the second speaker. "Soldier, you will follow orders."

"What the fuck you talking about?" the man said. "I'm out of here."

Crazy Mike drew down on him, "We will have no more de-serters. This man"—he motioned to the body of Ugly Bud— "aided and abetted the enemy. He had to be punished."

In an ever-widening circle, the other bikers began to back away. Foamy spittle hung on the corners of their leader's mouth and a maniacal light filled his eyes. It was his laugh that chilled their blood. When he threw his head back and opened his mouth, a wild disjointed howl issued forth. "Charge!" he yelled, taking off toward the swamp.

They watched him go and shook their heads. "The guy is whacked," Stinky said. "I feel a long ride coming on." The other bikers murmured in assent and headed for the road that led to the freeway.

*　　*　　*

MACE'S radio crackled. The dispatcher informed him that he was being patched through to Bob Marshall.

"It looks like our cases crossed," Bob said.

"Have you heard from your operative?"

"He called five minutes ago from the Satan's Pride clubhouse. Meet me there. He said they kidnapped some girl and thinks something big is about to go down."

"Where's the clubhouse?"

Bob gave him hurried directions.

Cassiletti had been at the station when Mace first called and he had hitched a ride over with the backup units dispatched to help. He brought with him the Teletype from Nan. Mace threw it in the backseat and briefed Cassiletti on the kidnapping. They walked around to the trunk and grabbed their Kevlar vests. While they strapped them on, a helmeted officer issued them shotguns. When the call had come in of a hostage situation, combined with "Officer needs assistance," the Special Operations Bureau was notified. The lieutenant in charge of SOB now set up a command center and deployed his teams of SWAT sharpshooters. He had also brought a hostage negotiator. The lieutenant briefed his men that the suspects were armed and extremely dangerous. Within eighteen minutes of the undercover DEA agent's first call, twelve police units were on the scene. Ernie arrived in an unmarked Ford. Helicopters were dispatched and local ham-radio enthusiasts tuned to police frequencies learned that something big was under way.

When the officers arrived at the clubhouse, they all found the same thing: disabled motorcycles, puddles of oil and gasoline, and a smear of bloody mud ending in a trail of swept dirt. No bikers, no hostage, no agent.

Mace bent down and studied the blood in the dirt. He glanced up and tracked the swept ground. The trail pointed toward a thick patch of bamboo. The helicopter radioed that they spotted a single male on a motorcycle, dragging something that looked like a body.

CRAZY Mike dragged the carcass of the dead man toward the cover of the bush. The bike fishtailed in the sand, and to maintain control Crazy Mike was forced to grab the handlebars with both hands. Munch's body fell to the ground. She regained consciousness as the body of Ugly Bud dragged past her. She struggled to her feet and began loping away. Behind her, Crazy Mike grunted as he rolled the body to a spot where it would be concealed. The sound of incoming choppers galvanized him. He undid the chain attached to the back of his motorcycle and left it with the body. It was time to retrieve his prisoner and get back to friendly territory. He restarted his motorcycle, planted a boot in the ground, and executed a quick turn. It took only seconds to reach the girl. He grabbed her by the scruff of her coat and pulled her on his lap.

The wheels of the police cars bogged down in the sand and the officers approached on foot, squatting for cover behind sparse trees. The helicopter hovered overhead, a sharpshooter leaning out through its open cockpit.

The dust behind the motorcycle rose like a small hurricane as the knobby rear tire found traction. Heavy with sand, the cloud settled quickly. A gale-force wind, created by the whirling blades of the helicopter, flattened the bamboo and the body became visible. The dead man lay there faceup. The toes of his Fry boots pointed skyward and his untucked shirt filled like a sail that blew up around his chest. The eyes of the body were opened in shock; half the forehead was missing and caked with dirt and sand. The helicopter's spotlight swept the scene.

Bob Marshall, recognizing his man, spoke into the microphone clipped to the collar of his windbreaker. "Officer down."

Over the sound of the motorcycle's engine and the helicopter's blades, there was a click as nine shotgun breeches cocked.

The movement of Munch's head as it swung around caused the assembled police to pause. In that moment of hesitation, Crazy Mike seized the opportunity to head out for the maze of trees and buildings to the east of the wetlands. If he could make it to the warehouses and hangars, he would have a chance to escape. He threw his head back in a final laugh, then pointed his chopper eastward.

Crazy Mike headed for a bike trail that wound through a grove of willows. He shifted to fourth gear and the bike lurched forward.

He had just reached the beginning of the trail when his engine sputtered the first time. He gave the throttle a desperate twist, but it didn't help. The front cylinder quit firing; a second later, its rear twin followed suit. He stared down at the motor in disbelief, then hit his brakes. With twenty feet left to go, he made a quick tactical decision to abandon his prisoner and continue on foot. He ran ten feet before the first bullet entered his body, just below the Prez patch. He didn't go down. It was like some part of his brain refused to register that it was time to lie down and die. A deafening barrage of bullets followed, issued from shotguns, assault rifles, and .38 Police Specials. He ran five more feet before the gates of hell opened to him and welcomed him home.

There were a few more sharp cracks. The sand around Munch kicked up.

"Cease fire" was called out.

Mace dropped his still cool shotgun and wondered why he hadn't fired. That question, he decided, he would deal with later. His more immediate concern lay curled in a fetal position on the road ahead of him. He reached her first and knelt beside her. Gently, he pried her open from the tight ball she had drawn herself into. Working carefully, he pulled down the arms that covered her head and encouraged her to relax her knees from her chest. Someone handed him a flashlight and he searched her for signs of bleeding.

"It's okay," he told her as he worked over her. "It's over. He's dead."

"I'm all right," she said, coming to a sitting position. "Got a cigarette?"

He got her a smoke but had to hold her hand still to get it lit.

"I'm sorry." He brushed the dirt from her hair. "It wasn't supposed to go down like this."

She nodded at his words, wide-eyed, and looked around her as if she had just arrived on the planet.

He shined his flashlight in her eyes. Was one pupil larger than the other? Bright red blood leaked to her shirt from a wound on her cheek. Something glinted below her collar and caught his eye. He picked it up and held it in his fingers. It was a St. Jude medal.

"Did you get religion since I saw you last?"

She turned to him. He thought he saw recognition there.

"I guess I did."

"It was a miracle that his bike quit when it did."

She pulled an empty sugar dispenser from her pocket and smiled almost shyly. "Sometimes He likes a little help."

"What else you got in there?" He reached into her pocket. "Do you mind?"

She shrugged.

He pulled out some crumbled papers, a motel key, a vial of pills, standard fare.

"Antibiotics," she said.

He studied the bottle, the label said, "Daisy Signman. Ampicillin. Take four times a day till gone."

"Don't worry," he told her, "I don't care about drugs."

"I'm clean," she said, as if it was important he know that.

"Good for you."

"Yeah," she said. "So far, it's been a fucking picnic."

"We better get that cut taken care of. You're going to need stitches."

She was shaking violently now, having trouble finding her mouth with the cigarette. He held it to her lips and she took a grateful drag. "But you wanted to know—"

He wrapped his arms around her protectively and helped her

to her feet. He noticed the handcuffs around her wrist. "Somebody give me a key," he yelled behind him. "Hospital first, then we'll talk. You can tell me all about Crazy Mike."

"And the guy I got the gun from."

"Yeah, later." Poor kid, that knock to the head had sent her to queer street. He guided her to the waiting car.

Cassiletti joined him and produced a fresh pair of handcuffs. Mace waved them aside. "We won't need those." He put her in the back of the car and got in beside her. "You drive," he told his partner.

"Will you call my boss for me?" she asked. Her teeth chattered audibly. "Damn," she said, "I can't seem to stop. It's so cold here."

"Hang on, honey. We're almost there." He knew to keep her talking. "You got a job?"

"H-Happy J-Jack's—it's in the valley."

He smiled down at her. "Didn't quite make it to the country, huh?"

"N-not yet. I went to a rodeo."

"How was it?"

"Weird."

He laughed at that. He squeezed her hand and noted the grease under her fingernails, the tiny cuts on her knuckles. They were working hands. "Don't worry. We'll get this all straightened out. I meant what I said."

"I'm gonna take a little nap . . . so tired." Her voice began to slur.

"Hey." He jostled her. "Stay with me. See, there's the hospital. If you go to sleep on me, I'll have to fill out all those forms by myself."

"Put whatever you want down; they never check." She smiled wanly and her eyes closed.

The car jumped the curb in the emergency entrance.

"Watch it!" Mace barked at Cassiletti.

"You're gonna ruin your alignment," she said, eyes still closed.

Orderlies ran to the car with a wheelchair.

She grabbed his collar and pulled him to her. "Tell them I don't do drugs. I got ten days and I want to keep them."

"Don't worry. They'll take care of you."

He watched her being wheeled off to the emergency room. Cassiletti came up behind him, "What a crock, huh?"

"What?"

"When she said she didn't do drugs. Fucking hype."

"People change."

"That's not what you said before."

"Yeah, well maybe I was mistaken."

Cassiletti stared inside the doors of the hospital. "I guess it's over?"

"Is it?" Mace turned on the big man. They were standing on the curb at the entrance of the emergency room. A nurse came outside and asked them to stand clear. Before she went back inside, she smiled encouragingly and added, "Officers" in that way women have of letting a guy know that they'd be open to additional dialogue. Mace shook his head: The more things changed . . .

The two men walked a little way, till they were standing between a bench and the brick wall by the side of the building. Mace turned on Cassiletti. "How did the bikers know she'd be at the restaurant?" Cassiletti's back was to the wall and Mace stood close to him, till their noses almost touched. "You were the only one I told about the meeting."

Cassiletti's face drained of all expression: a poker face.

Mace jammed a finger in his chest, but Cassiletti had nowhere to go. "And the siren in the alley—you warned her on purpose." Spittle flew from his mouth when he said the word *purpose* and sprayed Cassiletti's face. The big man made no move to wipe it clean. "This isn't over. I want to know whom you told."

"Nothing personal." He held up his hands. "Ernie asked me to keep him informed."

Mace spun from the younger cop in disgust and stole a glance back into the emergency room. Ugly suspicions began forming in his mind. The curtain was still pulled around the bed they had put her in. He could see the doctor's legs as they surrounded her. He reached into his pocket and pulled out the prescription bottle he took from the girl. He should probably let the doctors know that she was on medication.

He went back to the car and got the Teletype Nan had sent him. She had scribbled a note that said, "Call Dr. Miller when you get a chance." Did she call him that in bed, too? He rubbed his eyes; he was tired of carrying so much anger.

They would probably be awhile yet at the hospital, so he decided to use the time productively. He fished a dime out of his pocket and dialed Dr. Miller's exchange. They took the number Mace was calling from and said they'd have *Doctor* return the call. "*Detective* will be waiting," Mace said.

He called his house. He needed to let Caroline know that he was going to be late. Seemed like old times.

His answering machine picked up. His outgoing message played out and when the chime sounded, he said, "Caroline, pick up."

She lifted the receiver and he waited through the feedback until she figured out how to turn off the machine.

"Mace . . ."

"Listen, I'm sorry. Something came up and I don't know when this will be over. I'm at the hospital with Munch. She took a knock to the head; she's going to need some stitches, but I think she'll be fine. She's a tough one."

"Just be careful. I'll be here waiting for you."

"I'd like that."

Three minutes later, the pay phone rang. It was Dr. Miller.

Mace said, "Thanks for your help. We caught the guy—the main one, anyhow."

"More than one?"

"Yeah, it was a motorcycle gang."

"Oh no, very unlikely. You are looking for an individual. Your offender would never belong to a group. He will be a loner. He will feel too superior to belong to a fraternity."

"Maybe you didn't hear me. I'm not talking Phi Beta Kappa; he was the president of a motorcycle gang. We got him. He's dead."

"President? No, you are mistaken. Your killer is not a leader. Perhaps an executive of some sort, but he lacks the social skills to command."

"Listen, Doc, really, I appreciate all your help, but I think you're off base. Let me talk to Nan."

"What makes you think she's here?"

"Call it a suspicious, paranoid hunch. Will you put her on?"

"All right." There was a pause, a hushed discussion, and then Nan came on the line.

"You caught the guy?" she asked.

"Your boyfriend doesn't think so. I was looking through the lists you sent me. One name ties into our investigation, Daisy Signman. Ring any bells?"

"No. Where was she treated?"

"Van Nuys."

He waited while she shuffled through her papers.

"Here it is," she said. "Hey, we need to find this girl. We sent a telegram to her address, but it came back to us. She was treated for gonorrhea, but the results of her lab work showed that she's carrying two separate strains. She needs to come back to the hospital and get another prescription."

"Why is that?"

"She's got that PPNG I was telling you about, and apparently she's very active. Mrs. Canopolis made a note on the Signman file. When Mrs. Canopolis asked the girl to make a list of sexual contacts . . ." Nan paused. "I shouldn't be telling you this."

"It won't go any further. Please, Nan, it's important."

"The Signman girl didn't know the names of most of the men she had been with. Isn't that sad? It says here that she called one guy 'Mr. Potato Head.' You know, like that kid's toy? The plastic potato that you can put different noses and faces on. According to Mrs. Canopolis's note, that's why she called him that. The girl said it was because he looked like the one with the bow tie and glasses you see on the box."

Mace felt the hackles rise on his back. What had Munch said? He told her that she didn't have to worry about Crazy Mike and the next thing she said was, "And the guy I got the gun from."

"Nan, I gotta go." He paused. "Listen, I want to tell you something."

"Yes?"

"Be happy."

"Thank you. . . . You, too."

He hung up and ran back into the emergency room. An upset nurse stopped him.

"I'd like to lodge a complaint against one of your officers," she said.

He pushed back the curtains surrounding the bed where he had left Munch.

It was empty.

"Where is she?" he demanded of the nurse.

"I told the detective that we wanted to keep her overnight for observation, that she shouldn't be moved. He was most insistent and very rude. Shouldn't he have had a female officer with him for transporting the prisoner?"

"Bald guy? Funny little mustache, big nose, bow tie?"

"Yes, that was the man."

"Did the girl say anything when she saw him?" He gripped the nurse's arms tightly.

"I think she knew him."

"Why do you say that?"

"When he entered the room, her eyes got real big, and she said, 'You!'—like they had met before. She seemed afraid."

He grabbed behind the nurses' counter for the phone there.

"Hey," an orderly began to object, but the words froze in his throat when he saw the determined look on the detective's face.

"Do I need to dial nine first?"

"No, sir."

Mace called his ex-wife again. "Nan, put Miller on."

The doctor got back on the line and Mace questioned him feverishly. "If the killer was about to be found out, where would he go?"

"Assuming he isn't dead?"

"Yes, yes. What would his next move be?"

"You must put yourself in the man's head. He considers himself the victim now. He has justified his acts and now he sees himself as persecuted. Perhaps, if he knows he has come to the end, he will return to the beginning."

"You're talking in riddles, Doc."

"He will want to return to a simpler time, where it all began for him."

"The first killing?"

"Or at least the first manifestation of his sadistic tendencies."

He went back outside, where Cassiletti waited for him. "Come on, you drive."

"Where are we going?"

"Head south."

26

As they drove down Lincoln, Mace filled in Cassiletti on his suspicions. The younger man gripped the steering wheel and listened.

"Didn't he grow up around here?" Cassiletti asked.

Mace nodded. "Palisades del Rey. That's where it began."

Without being told, Cassiletti attached the beacon to the roof of the car but left the siren off. At Culver, they turned right. The coroner's wagon was still there. They whizzed past. They turned off Vista del Mar at Sandpiper and climbed the hill.

The house wasn't difficult to spot. It stood alone with its broken windows and shriveled landscaping. A Ford was parked in the driveway.

Mace leapt from the passenger seat, not stopping to shut his door. He quickly placed a hand on the hood of the Ford and noted that the engine was still warm. He could smell fresh exhaust and hear the crackle of the muffler as it contracted.

The front door was unlocked. He entered cautiously, revolver drawn. Slowly, he walked down the front hall. Faded squares of paint marked the spots where pictures had once hung. The hall runner was stained and smelled of urine. He could make out wiring conduit through fist-sized holes in the drywall. The first door he pushed through led to a kitchen. Once-cheerful wallpaper peeled from the corners. The appliances had been yanked, leaving hollow tentacles of gas and water lines. He pushed on.

Cassiletti followed, surprisingly catlike for a man his size. Mace gestured with the barrel of his gun for the other man to check the upstairs bedrooms.

After Cassiletti was out of sight, Mace stood motionless and became one with his surroundings. He listened. He blocked out the noises around him that belonged there and strained to hear what did not.

There was a rustling noise—a jingling, a grunting. A whimper? It was coming from the floorboards. He crouched low and concentrated.

Next to where the refrigerator had stood, there was a door. There had to be a basement. He stayed low and moved slowly across the floor, every nerve open and receiving. He pushed the door open slowly and waited for his eyes to become accustomed to the dark. He felt for and found a wooden banister. Then cautiously, quietly, he felt for each step with his heel. The voice below got clearer. It was a man. Ernie. He was cursing, and laughing.

"Shit." He chuckled. "That was close, huh?"

He was speaking to what appeared to be a life-sized crucifix. As Mace's vision adapted, he saw that it wasn't a crucifix, but a body suspended in the air by chains. It was Munch. Her eyes were open and unseeing, her mouth slack. Underneath her was a child's wading pool, empty.

Ernie stood next to a workbench. His hand reached for a crank mechanism. It was a winch wrapped with the same chains that were secured to Munch's ankles. The chains snaked through a simple pulley system. They pulled simultaneously on her legs, spreading them apart. A similar system was attached to her wrists.

Mace put his hand on the butt of his gun. "Release her," he said, "now."

Potts's hand froze on the handle. He didn't turn around.

"Unlock that thing, you sick son of a bitch, or I'll drop you. Do it."

Potts flicked up the catch mechanism and the gears quickly unwound. Munch collapsed in a lifeless heap on the floor, like a puppet with its strings cut. "You finally got here," Potts said. "I called for backup fifteen minutes ago. Where the hell you guys been?"

"Save it, Ernie. I know."

"Hey, can I help it if the guys got away? Must have been those bikers. They're big on revenge. Did you put out an APB?" As he spoke, he turned slowly around. His face was calm, almost peaceful.

"I know," Mace said again.

"It ends here," Potts said. "You want the collar?" He threw his hands up in the air, palms open. "You got it." He made a dismissive gesture behind him. "Forget about the bitch; she's done."

"Don't make me do this," Mace said through clenched teeth, more of a plea than a command. His revolver was out of the holster now.

Potts held up a hand, as if he was greeting a buddy at a beer hall. He smiled almost lazily, but his eyes remained calculating. "Relax, buddy. What do you care? She's a waste. You've seen her rap sheet. I'm doing her a favor." As he spoke, he gestured wildly. The sentences came more rapidly now, but his eyes never reflected panic or fear—just a cold calculation as he poked around the underbelly of Mace's psyche. "I'm a brother; I'm a cop. Look at yourself. What are you doing? You gonna shoot me? You didn't even shoot that asshole biker. You're not gonna shoot. You know better. Hey, if we don't got each other, who do we got? You're a shoo-in for lieutenant. Won't your dad be proud? How is Digger? Let me be the first to congratulate you."

He actually stuck out his hand.

"You're right: It's over." Mace's hand, holding the gun, trembled. Potts made a quick ducking move, a feint, testing Mace's resolve. Mace's hand steadied. "Don't make me do this."

"Lighten up, buddy. Nobody's doing anything." The hands

windmilled through the air in front of him, punctuating each word.

Mace took a step backward and glanced up the stairs. For an instant, he looked away. When he checked back on Ernie, his bowels constricted.

Ernie was holding a big .357. There would be no misses at this range.

The weapon filled the room.

It cocked.

The finger squeezed the trigger back.

Mace's gun began to swing back into position, seeming to lead his hands. But he knew he was too late. The doubt spun by Ernie's web of lies had defeated him. His hesitation cost him. He steeled himself for the hot blast, staring into the face of his executioner. The world froze, then began again in an excruciating state of slow motion.

Mace saw everything in minute detail, frozen frame by frame. Yet oddly, he wasn't afraid. There was no time to be afraid, no last words, just Ernie's soulless eyes, black and cold. Ernie's lips raised slowly on one side in a satisfied smirk, then formed "So stupid" as he cocked his head to one side. The words reached Mace at reduced speed, like a 33 record played at 78. The gun raised another inch. Mace stared down the cold black barrel. His death would come from there and nothing would ever matter again. It had already started.

Would his dad even remember that he had had a son? Was there any mark on the world left by the event of Mace's small life? Had he ever lived?

Mace looked back to Ernie's face. A new expression appeared there. He was not angry, or happy—merely surprised. Unbelievably, his hands released their grip on his weapon. His mouth formed a round O, and then he fell forward. A pair of surgical scissors were planted between his shoulder blades.

When he fell, another figure rose behind him, hair askew, eyes wild.

Munch.

Her arms were still stretched out in front of her, hands clasped together, almost as if she had been praying. Tears streamed down her face and then sound returned to the world. She was screaming, an animal keen of mortal passion. As she screamed, she kicked the body lying in front of her. The sound rushed from her in a fury that all ran together, like an ancient chant. "IATEU. IATEU." Her words began to separate in distinguishable syllables. She was yelling, "I hate you. I hate you," over and over again, punctuating the word *hate* with a kick to his head.

Mace let her go, till she had wound herself down. Let all that venom leech from her tiny form. He was there to catch her when she slumped to the floor. He rubbed her wrists where the chains had bitten into her.

"It's over. It's over." He kept repeating the words as he smoothed back her hair. The ER doctor had sutured the cut on her cheek with black thread. Her nose swelled between two blackening eyes. But her eyes were clear and very much alive. He pulled her to him. "I'm sorry. I'm sorry I couldn't stop him sooner."

"It's okay," she assured him. "Like my sponsor always says, 'Welcome to the human race.'"

Cassiletti appeared on the landing at the top of the stairs. "Everything all right?" he called down.

"We're going to need a wagon," Mace said. "And the CS crew. Cassiletti, get the tape. I don't want anything disturbed."

"Am I under arrest?" Munch asked.

"No, babe, what we got here is a clear case of HVA." He helped her up and wrapped a supporting arm around her shoulders. She was so thin. He could feel her bones through the fabric of her blouse. Her hair smelled of anise and sagebrush, the wild spices of the wetlands. "I understand that you're quite a mechanic. Ever work on a train before?"

27

After a long evening at the station, filling out reports and having depositions taken, Munch explained the events that had led up to the death of her father, the unlamented Flower George.

"He sold me to those assholes for a bag of speed. He didn't even like speed." She wiped her nose with her sleeve. "When they got through with me, they were going to sell me again—to Mr. Potato Head. I'd been with the guy before; he wanted to stick a flashlight up me. I bit his hand and ran away."

"Where did that happen?" Mace asked.

"He had a van. We were parked by the beach. After that, all the working girls knew to avoid that van. I wasn't the only one."

"How did he know the bikers?" Captain Divine asked. Mace had called him at home to be in on the debriefing.

"Crazy Mike had something on him."

"How do you know that?" Mace asked.

She shrugged her shoulders and blew at the mug of coffee cupped in her hands. "Just the way they talked to each other. Mr. Potato Head didn't seem like the kind of guy to hang out with bikers, so I figured it was some sort of business thing. I overheard them talking and Crazy Mike said something—like 'You've been getting sloppy. They found the last one, made it hot for everybody.' Potato Head said that that wouldn't happen again. Sounded like there had been others."

"Sounds like Crazy Mike caught Ernie cleaning up after one of his parties. No wonder Crazy Mike had no record," Mace said. Divine nodded.

A secretary walked into the room with a sketch pad. Cassiletti took it from her and thanked her. Mace watched him. Cassiletti seemed to have aged twenty years in the last two hours; his boyish innocence had evaporated. It wasn't his fault. Ernie'd had them all fooled.

"So what happened after you realized that the Pride was going to hand you over to Potts?" Captain Divine prompted.

"They thought I was passed out, so they left me alone in the loft. I could see and hear them talking through the slats in the ceiling. Your guy Potts was asking Mike for a girl no one would miss. Crazy Mike said he had just the one, but he told him it would cost a gram of heroin to keep my old man quiet. That Potts guy went out to his car and came back with a glassine bag full of China White. God, I was pissed. You think Flower George was gonna save any of that for me? Not on your life."

The men didn't know what to say to that. Cassiletti handed Mace the pad of paper. It was the composite sketch of the hooker basher plaguing Venice—aka Homicide Detective Ernest Potts. Mace handed the sketch to the captain and Munch resumed her narration.

"Then it hit me. This guy was going to snuff me." She sipped her coffee. Mace noted that her hands still shook. "They came up to get me and thought I was still passed out. I just made myself go totally limp. Even when they kicked me, I didn't react. They picked me up and dumped me in the trunk of Potts's car. It was lucky he wasn't driving the van."

"Why is that?" Mace asked.

"He wouldn't have been so careless if I'd been in the van with him. Knowing I was locked in the trunk gave him a false sense of security. Trunks are meant to be safe from the outside," Munch told the men assembled around her in the squad room. "They're pretty easy to open from the inside."

"And the gun?" Mace asked.

"The idiot left it in his jacket in the trunk." Munch gave an embarrassed shrug. "Before I escaped, I went through his pockets. Habit." She grinned and the men laughed.

"So then you went back to the house on Brooks?" Mace prompted.

"First I stopped at a friend's house and got down. That was the last time I ever used. I didn't even feel it. I don't think I was feeling anything. I wanted to tell George what those guys were going to do to me. I wanted him, for once, to say he was sorry. He never did. When I got there, he was OD'd on the bed, but he saved me a taste. It was still in the syringe left in his arm. I pulled it out. . . ."

"The syringe?" Mace asked.

"Yeah."

"Did it bleed, his arm?"

"I don't think so."

"Think—it's important." He leaned forward and grasped her hand. "Did blood pump out when you pulled the needle out of his vein?"

"No. No, it didn't. I pulled it out and I went in the bathroom and tied off. Just before I fixed, I looked at myself in the mirror. And I knew. It was him or me. It was like all the rage caught up to me, all of it—everything that had just happened, everything that had happened before, everything that was yet to happen. I threw down the syringe and I grabbed the gun. He was still lying there, naked and stinking, like everything evil and disgusting in this world."

"And already dead," Mace said quietly.

She stopped, stunned, and stared at him.

"You shot him, honey. I know that. But you shot a dead man."

"So what happens now?" she asked.

Mace stood up and walked across the room. He picked up the

eraser and offered it to his captain. Divine nodded his head and took the eraser from Mace. Then he turned to the board and made the name Mancini, written in red, disappear.

"I guess you better get back to the valley," Mace said to Munch. "You're gonna need your sleep if you're going to be worth a damn at work tomorrow."

Cassiletti grabbed the car keys off the desk. "I'll give her a ride." He turned back to Mace. "I'll put in for a transfer in the morning. I really let you down. I'm sorry."

"Hey, he had us all fooled. You can't quit now. Shit, I almost died raising you. You can't let all that effort go to waste."

Cassiletti smiled tentatively. Mace laid a hand on the big man's shoulder. "I think we're going to call you Tiger," Mace said. "Tony the Tiger."